The
Strangers *of*
Braamfontein

Praise for *The Strangers of Braamfontein*

"Gripping, fast-paced, no holds barred. This story about life on the streets of Braamfontein is uncompromising in its depiction of the drugs, sex and gang rivarly that often threatens to consume all of those involved. It also reminds us of how the quests for a better life elsewhere often ends in unmitigated tragedy and how a country's dysfunction feeds this desperation."

– Nze Sylva Ifedigbo,
author of *Believers and Hustlers*

"Onyeka Nwelue's The Strangers of Braamfontein is heavily peopled with characters as dark as the night who are cohabiting in a brutal place where death is cheap. Raw, gritty, fast-paced, this is not a book you can glance through because it will force you to keep turning the pages. It will make you shiver with trepidation. It is such a searing read. This is a book to love."

– OlukoredeYishau,
author of *Vaults of Secrets and
In The Name of Our Father*

"*The Strangers of Braamfontein* is the story of life on the rough side in Lagos and Johannesburg. An interesting and bizarre take on violence."

– JAMES CURREY

"Nwelue's fast-paced novel is a raw and hard-eyed dive into a dark world peopled with characters for whom survival comes at a cost. Bold and daring, *The Strangers of Braamfontein* explores all the ways in which life can crush us."

– Chika Unigwe,

author of *On Black Sisters' Street*

"Funny, lively and compelling characters, Onyeka Nwelue's *The Strangers of Braamfontein* is a memorable read."

– Jumoke Verissimo,

author of *A Small Silence*

THE STRANGERS OF BRAAMFONTEIN is the newest novel by Onyeka Nwelue, and wow, not only is it new but it surpasses all of his other novels in its gritty descriptions of violence, murder, all kinds of sex, drugs, bigotry ...... the list goes on .... and on.

"There is a danger in a single story, so says Chimamanda Adichie, for a single story "creates stereotypes. And the problem is not that they are untrue but that they are incomplete. They make one story become the only story." In this novel the stereotypes abound: the Nigerian gangsters and drug dealers, the South African criminals and corrupt policemen, the

Congolese murderers, the Francophone vicious and terrifying mobsters and the prostitutes, both male and female, of every nationality. These stereotypes are true, but Nwelue, also gives his characters other personality traits, empathy, sadness, love, fear, and so while they may live the stereotypical story we learn that this is not only what they are. They are real people with real flaws; real goodness and real toughness. In the novel Nwelue also shows us bigotry and what it does – it kills. Bigotry literally kills, but it also kills community, connection and an appreciation of another. The prejudices that are in the novel range from homophobia, xenophobia and misogyny. These prejudices are, he shows us, the product of fear, not so much the fear of the other, but the fear of oneself.

What a novel. I want to read it again."

– Barbara Adair,
author of *In Tangier We Killed the Blue Parrot*

"Onyeka Nwelue's *THE STRANGERS OF BRAAMFONTEIN* is a very timely novel that casts a light on a story rarely accounted for in modern fiction: the travails of African immigrants, not in Europe or elsewhere, but within Africa. Nwelue's portrayal of characters in extremis is shot through with such underhanded humor and wisdom that echoes the

novels of Kurt Vonneghurt. A bold and entertaining novel by a very promising talent."
– Chigozie Obioma,
two-time Booker Prize shortlisted
author of *The Fishermen* and *An Orchestra of Minorities*

"A vivid portrayal of lives rocked by hardship and crime across two megacities, and a provocative tale about survival."
– Chioma Okereke,
 author of Bitterleaf

"There's so much to love with Nwelue's The Strangers of Braamfontein; the complex and varied characters; the ever-evolving plot; Osas the primary character in whose eyes we discover the underbelly of Braamfontein, one of Johannesburg's central suburbs and, Nwelue's keen sense of observation and his understanding of human desperation. For me, personally, I applaud Nwelue's narration and language in unfolding this high-octane drama that examines the lives of immigrants searching for second chances in one of Africa's most diverse cities."
– Jude Dibia,
author of Walking with Shadows

ONYEKA NWELUE

The Strangers of Braamfontein

Abibiman
Publishing

New York & London

First published in Great Britain in 2021 by
Abibiman Publishing
www.abibimanpublishing.com

All rights reserved. Published in the United Kingdom
by Abibiman Publishing, an imprint of
Abibiman Music & Publishing, London.

Abibiman Publishing is registered under Hudics LLC in the
United States and in the United Kingdom.

ISBN: 978-1-9989958-0-6

Cover design by Fred Martins
Author photograph: Lidudumalingani

Printed in the United Kingdom by Clays Ltd.

To
Professor WOLE SOYINKA,
My teacher

And
Professor LESLYE OBIORA,
My other teacher

Death has made war upon our house.
 • Kofi Awoonor,
    "Songs of Sorrow"

CONTENTS

INTROIT

Braamfontein roused itself to life like a child reluctant to face a school day. The morning sun peeked behind the curtains of the clouds, gradually presenting itself one shaft at a time until it stood in its full glory. But Braamfontein and its people never appeared to notice. Blocks of apartment and commercial buildings, most of which stood out in different stages of disrepair, sprawled across the landscape in defiance of beauty. And the people too, went about whatever gave them food and keep, caring for nothing else.

Ruth sat on a bench by a deserted park, watching the world go by, taking note of this stranger and that. She could tell the ones who were hurrying off to work at some office or factory; those ones weren't hard to make out. From the way they dressed, their composure and the urgency in their pace, she could guess how much importance each one had in their places of work. It struck her to realize that most of them occupied the lowest rungs of the corporate

ladder with the way they hurried along. There were
the ones who idled on, taking their time, sometimes
with hands dug into their pockets, and no clear
destination in mind. These ones were mostly boys
and men. Thieves and pickpockets looking for an
easy pick. And there were the small-time drug dealers
too, looking out for anyone interested in buying pills.
Braamfontein!

A lady hurried along. She looked Indian. Ruth
could not take her eyes off her. There was no way she
could mistake a prostitute when she saw one. In that
moment, she wondered if the lady was returning late
from a client's place. There was no way she would
accept such behaviour from any of her girls. Almost
at once, she cringed and looked away as a feeling of
guilt hit her. Thinking about the Indian prostitute
had brought on a wave of emotions she was trying
to stave off.

News had gotten to her of the murder of a
prostitute in an apartment uptown. The deceased
had been one of her girls and the killer was still at
large. On asking around, she had found out that
the girl had become too familiar with a particular
customer, a pink man who was said to have some
money and probably had a drug problem. The news

had made her so angry that she had flung her phone against the wall of her apartment and had had to come out in the open, to some place far away from her house and neighbourhood, to clear her head before she smashed more valuable things. Why would the girl be so stupid to flout a simple rule that she took the time to instill in them? 'Business is business,' she would always say. "A prostitute can't afford the luxury of romance while in the game. It is too *damned* dangerous."

She sighed.

She knew she would have to have another talk with the girls, to make them learn from what has just happened. That way, she would straighten them up in case there were any of them still entertaining any stupid ideas about romance and a *happily ever after* with clients.

Ruth raised her eyes just in time to catch the gaze of a bearded man in the distance. He looked away immediately and leaned against the wall at a corner, pretending not to be interested in her. She sized him up. His mismatched yellow socks peeked out of the hem of his crumpled undersized chinos trousers and he appeared to have slept for many days in his denim jacket.

Time to get going, Ruth said to herself. It was to an unpredictable part of Braamfontein she had come to.

Getting off her seat, she strode briskly to the road, flagged down a taxi and climbed in before calling out her destination to the driver.

Part 1

BAPTISM

The Negro has suffered far more from the commission of this crime against the women of his race by white men than the white race has ever suffered through his crimes.
— Ida B. Wells

SHARP GUYS

The urban sprawl of Johannesburg city centre is such that nobody knows where the pink man had come from. Those who were questioned later, who had seen him pull up outside the building where the girl lived, were not even sure of the make or model of his car. The witnesses did remember him as an impressively dressed pink man though, but with a face too ordinary and therefore too difficult to describe. One witness recalled him at the wheel of his car, glancing now and then at his wristwatch, as though he had somewhere important to be; and then looking out of the car and down the road, with a nasty scowl.

Soon, the girl approached the car. Her skin was so dark that she could be considered Kenyan. Her long legs bore her bony frame with elegance. She left her building the same way each day, bearing a small travel bag, and ducking into the passenger seat next to the driver of the non-descript car. They would set off immediately. It was always the same pink man behind the wheel, the witnesses recalled. Just as no one knew where the man came from, no one knew where the two of them went. It was as though they materialised before everyone then dissolved into thin air.

There was another witness, a dumpy woman with droopy cheeks. She said she had once seen the girl and the man at a hypermarket. They were buying the usual stuff, like anybody else, and while the man smiled at the cashier, the girl's face had been as blank as the gleaming supermarket floor. That was all Mrs Dumpy could recall before she excused herself to purchase baby clothes for her pregnant daughter.

The building caretaker from across the street said he had seen the girl return to her flat with the pink chap. He had been fixing a broken pipe as he watched the girl and the man have dinner at her kitchen table.

"The window of the room was open, so I saw everything," he said, smiling proudly and revealing a set of broken teeth. When the curtains were finally closed, he admitted that he saw nothing more.

That was all the detectives gathered from the residents. They wondered if this girl, who had moved in three weeks ago and whose name nobody knew, was the pink man's mistress. This was Braamfontein, after all. It was not strange for the girls living there to try snare affluent pink men with their cunts. The street cleaners said they saw the pink man leave the apartment one Wednesday morning, just as the sunlight broke into the new day. There was nothing remarkable about him or about how he walked. They said he had gotten into the car, turned on the ignition, and driven into the dawn.

This was as much that could be gathered on the matter from Jorissen Street, with its bustle and tall buildings.

Not a soul had observed how someone had breezed into the building on that Wednesday morning and knocked on her door.

Not a soul had been there to notice that the girl, in a night robe and with a steaming teacup in hand, had opened the door.

Only the killer had borne witness to the gunfire that preceded the smash of the teacup hitting the ground. Only the killer had seen the girl turn cold and lifeless with eyes glazed over, blood and brain splattered on the small living room wall.

It is the early hours of dawn when darkness gradually surrenders to the light of day. An aura of gloom rests over the small standalone Emerald Escorts building famed for housing Nigerians.

A little walk down the poorly tarred road and one would get to an abandoned textile factory, which was always littered with condoms, burnt leaves and plastic. The air is chilly. It had just drizzled, and the emerging sunlight glints off the droplets on the sidewalk.

In a poorly lit room on the right-wing of the Emerald Escorts building, three girls in loud, multi-coloured hairstyles sit on chairs in a semi-circle. The room has one pink abstract print above the bed. A full-length mirror takes up a section of the wall. A pronounced crack runs down the entire length of the room, from the lone window to the ceiling.

One of the girls is biting her nails. They call her April. She is fair and plump. Esther is seated in the middle, her face meditative as she fingers her rosary. The other one is Ese. She is short and has a large bosom. A burning cigarette sticks out of Ese's mouth, and she only attends to it when she needs to puff out smoke and flick off some ash. She seems to have her mind removed from the room.

April shakes her head, as though to jiggle away the disturbing thoughts. "This life, na wa o. Na the very last thing wey I expect hear dis morning."

Esther sighs. "I dey tell you, babe. This thing still dey shock me. The only good thing be say, where she dey better pass here."

"Fuck that shit," Ese fires at her, startling the two girls with her outburst. "Better pass where? How you take dey reason, sef? So e go better say you die than say you dey for Emerald? Nonsense!"

"No be so I take mean am," Esther says, almost apologetically. "Wetin I mean be say, at least she don finally rest."

Ese glares at her. "And wetin that one come mean na? Them kill person, you say she don go rest."

Just as April begins to shake her head, Esther claps at her. "Abeg abeg abeg, keep that your mouth one side oh. Na me kill am?"

"I talk say na you?" Ese retorts.

Slowly, April rises to her feet. "Girls, abeg, this one no be time for this kind thing na. No be time for quarrel be this. Make una calm down, jare."

"Na me start am?" Esther argues. "No be madam *fuck you* start noise?"

Ese rolls her eyes, as she lights another cigarette. "Now no be time to start quarrel, I take God beg una," April says, throwing pleading glances at them.

Esther hisses sardonically, continues kneading her rosary.

"Wetin police even talk about de matter sef?"A voice enquires, startling the girls. There is a woman standing in the doorway. She is beautiful, probably in her mid-thirties. Her newly made eyelashes stand out thick, weighing down on her eyelids. Everyone knows her—Madam Ruth. The air of authority she exudes commands so much respect that none of her girls meets her gaze. Like a predator in conquered territory, she steps into the room. The girls are too intimidated to speak. They had not been expecting her sudden appearance.

"The girl don go," she says, not looking at them. "Police go do their work. Una no dey plan do una own today?"

The girls discreetly exchange glances. Their heads are lowered in guilt.

"Make una no reason that girl matter. Na so the world be." She halts before the mirror and stares into it. "Here today, gone tomorrow, na so we see am." She lets out a heavy sigh. "Make una ready for work this night, holiday no dey."

She turns to leave but pauses, thinking one of the girls had muttered under their breath. In a flash, she spins around, facing the girls. They all look innocent as lambs. Perhaps the muttering had not come from them. Is her mind playing tricks? Perhaps it has something to do with the news of the dead girl. She used to be one of her most valuable possessions. Maybe it is guilt. No, not possible. She had outgrown such feeble emotions long ago. Her girls are old enough; they should understand what they are getting themselves into.

She nods at them and leaves. They are good girls, not the types who would gossip or mutter behind her back. Never, for once, had they given her trouble and they should not. She had picked them up from the filth, brushed off the dirt, and groomed them into treasures, irresistible to a man and his pockets. She does not care what others think, but she always likes to see herself as a curator gathering abandoned artefacts and polishing them until they became invaluable. Even though she has been putting it off, one day she will have to tell these girls her own story. She will explain to them the flames that licked her soul, melted it, and forged her into Madam Ruth.

Osas has just stepped outside and walked a few meters from the gym where he had gone to see Andre when he thinks he is being followed. At first, he thinks it is Andre. Perhaps the fellow had forgotten to tell him something and needed to do so immediately. When he turns around, he sees two men in a respectable distance. They notice him turn around and try to look disinterested but he sees through their act. Something about the men does not sit right. Surely, they are not thugs; they look too collected for that. Their carriage, the air of authority on them, their attempt to conceal their presence and blend in, all pointed to one thing. Surely, there is no way he could mistake a police officer in a crowd even if the officer was in plainclothes. Something about them always gives them away, and most definitely, these two are police officers and they have their attention on him.

For a moment, he considers breaking into a run, but then he ditches the idea. What about ducking in a corner and evading them? The idea seems appealing. He will have to maintain his normal stride until he gets to the end of the block where he will evade them. Then, what could they have on him? Has someone tipped him off, or what? It is a good thing he did not have any drug on him. His mind raced to the possible things he may have done wrong in the past few days. There are quite a few of them and he had been careful while at them. He makes a silent prayer and concentrates on getting to the end of the block while maintaining his calm.

"Hey!"

His heart sinks. He pretends not to hear.

"Stop there, you!"

They hasten up and draw closer, but he pretends to not to hear or notice they are talking to him. A woman approaching him looks apprehensive at first and then signals to him that he is being addressed. With this, he knows that there is no need pretending any further if he is to maintain his cool. Cursing the woman in his heart, he halts, turns around and waits for the men to stroll up to him.

"Good evening, sirs" he greets them. Almost immediately, he chides himself for offering a greeting. A stupid thing to do under the circumstance, he thinks to himself. The men do not reply him. They stand in an imposing manner before him, a calculated attempt aimed at subtle intimidation. One of them is burly, and the other a little trim. They are South Africans.

"Where are you from?"The burly one asks.

"Nigeria."

The men exchange knowing glances. "And what does your name happen to be?"

"Oscar."

"Interesting."

"Can I have an ID?"The trim one asks.

Osas fetches in his pocket for his passport, all the while wishing that his hands remained steady. If they had given him a handshake, they would have noticed how sweaty his palms were but good a thing they had not.

The burly one takes his passport and flips through the pages with disinterest. In the same manner, he hands it back. "Where do you live?" He asks.

Osas feels a wave of relief. They had nothing on him. They must have singled him out at random, and as long as he does not appear suspicious, they will let him go.

"I live on Bicard Street. Number 35"

The burly one shifts his weight to one foot. He seems to have run out of ideas. Maybe it is a sort of cue for the slim one to come in. "You're Nigerian, I see."

"Yes," Osas replies.

"Okay," he treats Osas to a quiet stare as though contemplating what next to say. "There's a murder uptown. A Nigerian. A prostitute, actually. She was murdered in an apartment. I am sure you have heard about it. Do you happen to know anything about it?"

Osas shakes his head.

The detectives stare down at him as though in search of a hint from his countenance. Whatever it is they are looking for, Osas swears in his heart never to give it to them. These ones are bullies, and he sure knows how to handle such as them. He does not know the girl they are asking after.

He had heard the story as everyone else has but there was no way he was going to tell these bullies that the girl was one of Madam Ruth's girls.

"These foreigners," the burly one says, shaking his head. He taps his partner on the arm, and they move away.

Osas stands, looking at them. They stroll back the road they had come. They never even give a backward glance in his direction. He turns, continues his walk, rounds a street corner and tells himself to get the incidence off his mind. There is so much waiting to be done, and an incidence of futile intimidation is not something to take seriously.

"How far, my guy?"

Osas looks up from his work on the sink to see Dayo walk towards him in the small kitchen. His earrings on his left ear glint in the overhead fluorescent lights. "Fine," Osas replies. "Good morning."

Dayo walks past him, tapping him in the ass. Osas flinches, nearly dropping a dinner plate. His first impulse is to charge at the head chef. This is the third time the older man has done this. It makes Osas cringe, how Dayo always makes body contact when showing him a thing or two to do for him in the restaurant kitchen.

Osas does not do anything. He does not charge at the head chef, nor deals him any blows. Not even a word parts his lips. It is not worth it. He is lucky to have even gotten this job a week after arriving in South Africa. He would not jeopardise this on some man who is already turning grey all over, wears an earring, and is obviously into men. It was better to lay low until something more appealing comes up.

He turns his attention to the stack of plates on the sink. Work is not looking especially good this morning. The heater has been turned off. They say it is faulty, but there are no signs of it being repaired yet. His hands feel numb from being soaked in cold water for the last three hours. It has been a busy morning so far, and the dishes keep piling up. At this rate, he will have his hands in the chilly water for at least another three hours. His legs ache from standing. He wishes for the evening to come when he can close up for the day.

It had not been like this in the beginning, when he got this job at the De Bliss Grub and Pub. The owner is Nigerian, and he had looked understanding. He had not asked for much documentation, only a copy of his passport and address. If you are a good person and hardworking, the proprietor had told him, you would make it in South Africa; and can even start an establishment of your own. The pay had seemed good, too. There was always extra food. However, things began to look different shortly afterwards. Some of the staff began to quit, and Osas could see why. The proprietor delayed the payments and treated his employees rudely, except towards the end of the month, when he would talk sweet to them. None of the works had yet been replaced, so Osas was left to occupy more than just his dishwasher role. He had been working such long hours that there was neither energy nor time to scout for new jobs.

"Osas."

Osas looks up from the dishes as his mind jolts back to reality. It is the proprietor, standing at the doorway.

"Come."

Osas rinses his hands and wipes them on his apron.

"No. Remove your apron and headwear. Quick! You are going to help at the lobby. The pressure is too much there. Fast fast! Don't be lazy."

Osas gulps down the anger rising in his throat. It makes his eyes water and his fingers quiver. The proprietor does not notice. Osas removes his apron and headwear, secures them on a hook and leaves, following the proprietor out of the kitchen and into the small hallway leading to the lobby.

The lobby is busy. Almost every table is occupied, except for a few littered with used trays and plates with leftovers. A little crowd of teenagers gathered in front of the service counter, giving their orders. A trained industry eye can see that the three boys behind the counter are hiding their mounting stress fairly well. There is a pool table to one end of the lobby. South Africans are always playing because it is an unspoken rule that Nigerians stay off it. They only come into the restaurant to eat and drink, and then they leave. The pool table end of the lobby looks isolated, and the shabbiness of the South Africans makes that part dingier. The muted TV screens on the walls at strategic corners of the lobby are tuned to MTV Base. Soft Nigerian music filter in from overhead speakers.

"Clear the tables," the proprietor whispers to Osas, before heading off in the direction of his small office.

Osas gets to work.

He clears three tables and when he gets to an unoccupied table, he stops to contemplate for a moment. The burger pack on the tray is as untouched as the carton of fruit juice.

"Leave am," a confident voice says behind him.

Startled, Osas steps aside. The man who had spoken is young, a little older than Osas, wearing a thin gold chain that stands out among his other articles of clothing. He looks well to do and carries himself as such. You cannot but recognise a Nigerian when you see one, wherever you may be. The young man wipes his hands with a paper towel as he settles into his seat. He must have come from the restroom. Perhaps it is not the restroom; he may have gone to wash his hands at any one of the sinks built into the walls at strategic parts of the restaurant lobby.

Osas feels clumsy. "Sorry," he says, and walks off to attend to another table at the farthest end that a woman and her three noisy kids have just vacated. He cannot stop stealing glances at the young

Nigerian. This is how he should be; he keeps saying to himself, as he cleans the table, takes the dishes into the kitchen, adds them to the waiting pile on the sink, and returns to the lobby.

He does not like being in the lobby because it always makes him feel inadequate seeing other immigrants doing well. Yes, he is new to South Africa, he will have to give himself time to experience and grow. However, he is not keen to hear these admonitions. He does not want to hear them at all. Such words kill and dampen the spirits. There are homeless immigrants in Braamfontein, as there are in Johannesburg. He had seen them on the streets. The sight had scared him. They still do. Possibly these ones had been listening to the dampening admonitions. They may still be hoping. But not him. He would not follow their path. Back in Nigeria, did not they say *no time* as if it were a slogan? Yes, no time at all. He had come to South Africa to make something of his life and he will. No time.

The young man eats and talks on the phone. He speaks a lot of Igbo and a little Pidgin English. It sounds like he is discussing business. Who knows what business he is into? Probably drugs. So many run the business here. Everyone says it pays very well. He had heard the stories back in Nigeria.

The young man seems angry. His face says as much, and his gestures too. A piece of the burger spills out onto his shirt. He reaches for his handkerchief and scrubs at the ugly stain while keeping the phone steady against his ear, propped on his shoulder. He is so distracted that he does not notice one of the South Africans from the pool table section; snatch his wallet from the table on his way out.

Osas does not stop to think. He covers the space between himself and the South African and grabs him by the arm. The South African turns around with a nasty look on his face. Maybe it is the frustration of his futile toils at the restaurant or his dislike for the shabbily dressed South Africans who throw their weight around like every immigrant owes them the very air they breathe, but Osas punches the man in the face so hard that he falls to the floor. He reaches into the man's baggy shorts and retrieves the wallet. Straightening, he finds every eye fixed on him. The thief stands, holding onto his bloody nose, spits viciously on the floor and stomps away. His friends have seen the drama. They make jokes of it among themselves, laugh and return to their pool tables.

A hand taps Osas on the shoulder. It is the owner of the wallet. He holds out a hand. Osas puts the wallet in it. The young man pockets his wallet and holds out his hand again. It is an invitation to a handshake. Osas takes his hand.

"You na correct guy. Wetin them dey call you?"

"Osas."

"You be Edo boy."

"Yes."

"Sharp guy. My name na Chike. E be like say you come new for this town?"

"Yes. I just come. I say make I dey manage for here until I see a person like you wey go show me the way."

Chike smiles. "Confirm."

"So how e dey be na? Which one be the way forward?"

"We go see another time. Pass me your digits."

"I never get phone number yet. Na my Naija Whatsapp number I still dey use."

"No wahala."

Osas says his number as Chike punches it into his phone. He saves it in his contact list.

"We go link up," Chike says.

"Thank you, bro."

They shake hands and Chike leaves in a hurry. Osas sets about clearing Chike's table. He is not surprised. The man is Igbo. Igbo people always make it quickly. He gathers the leftovers onto the tray. Much of the burger is left uneaten. The juice, untouched.

As Osas heads towards the kitchen, he wonders if his boss has noticed the fracas with the South African. He wonders if it will earn him any credits with his boss. Most importantly, he prays that the young man, Chike, keeps his word and calls him.

Benin City, where Osas was born, is known for historical relics. Wherever you turn, you see subtle evidence of a rich culture that had once been the envy of civilisations of a time long gone. Osas grew up in such environment, but of course, he took all of these for granted. To him, Benin City is just a city, and everything is as it should be. Aspects of Benin history always filtered into him, but who cared about such. He was a growing child who was trying to make sense of the world around him, which he considered unstable. Surely if he were to exert any efforts besides fending for his stomach, it had to be in the direction that would make him understand who his father and mother were and why he had to live with his grandmother. Other children were not in the same situation as he, but why him? It was better he figured these things out than bother himself with why the

Oba dressed in a certain way and all of those things that didn't in any way secure food and a promise of stability to him.

Things were to begin to change soon afterwards, when he began to overhear discussions with visitors to Benin City.

It struck him to realise that most visitors from other Nigerian cities regarded the relics of the Benin people as idolatrous. They said Benin was the headquarters of witches in Africa and that all the cultural relics proved this. For a moment, he began to try to make sense out of this. Something had happened earlier in the compound where he lived. A neighbour's child had gone crying to her mother.

"Mummy, Mama Ayo call me a witch."

The mother had looked up from her laundry. "Clean your eye," she had replied, "na witch dey sabi witch."

It could be true, after all. There were times when he heard strange noises on the roof at night. They scared him most of the time, but his grandma never seemed perturbed, and this had always put him at ease.

Maybe she knew so much of these things and he had not learned from her. Was there anything he learned from her, even? She hardly said anything that was not a nag or demeaning to his morale. There were times when he had woken with nail scratches on his body. She would examine them and would not say anything. Sometimes she made comments he could not make any sense of. Those nail marks on his body were mysterious. He wondered when he had scratched his skin so badly to leave those marks on it.

Someone had told him that witches made those marks on his skin, as they tasted his blood. Perhaps it was true, and his blood never tasted so well for them to have taken a sip or anything more than a little taste. Perhaps they came back every now and then to see if the taste of his blood had improved. It could have if his meals consisted of anything better than what his grandma grudgingly made available to him.

His newfound enlightenment came by way of conversations he had in the motor park. It began to make a lot of sense that Edo people were great craftsmen and sculptures from as far back as the early centuries when they had been an empire known all over the world and envied by the British and the Portuguese. It explained why Edo had the best carpenters and woodworkers, and why depictions of the bronze head were so important to the Edo people.

It was a masterpiece with intricate details. There were other works equally as intricate and masterful, and you saw evidence of them wherever you turned in Edo.

He learned about the ancient civilisation, that was the Benin Empire and its great walls. Someone said the British had attacked Benin, destroyed its famous city walls and carted away with its artefacts to Britain, to be displayed in museums. People paid to view the artefacts that are guarded and kept on display in British museums.

The very thought made Osas laugh; the thought that he would have to travel all the way to the UK, pay some money to see aspects of his culture that were stolen from his ancestors and proudly exploited. Very funny. If then he was to go to any of those museums and steal any of those artefacts would he be called a thief by the British people? It reminded him of something that had happened. A thief had broken into someone's house, but the owner of the house had noticed on time and raised the alarm. The thief had taken off, but the home owner had followed after the thief, shouting *thief! Thief!*

Just when people had begun to mill out of their houses to give pursuit, the thief had joined in the alarm and had pointed out the owner of the house.

By the time, everyone had realised the foul play, the homeowner had sustained some good deal of beating and the thief had been nowhere to be found.

Osas believed that those artefacts needed to be returned from the UK and everywhere else in Europe where they are being kept in museums. It did not make sense to him that you would take somebody's property and boldly hold it out for the person to see. It is bullying, and he had seen a lot of it, growing up.

It is six in the evening, and Osas closes for the day. The proprietor had asked him to work extra hours. Osas had murmured something about extra pay but the man had pretended not to hear, and Osas had returned to his work grudgingly. He is glad the hours have finally dragged past. He leaves the premises quickly, as though his sanity depended on it. Sure, it does. The farther away he gets from the restaurant, the better he starts to feel.

He walks towards the bus stop thinking about the urgent need to get another job. Maybe it is best never to work for a Nigerian employer; they still carry the wickedness they are known for back in Nigeria, like a snail hauling its own shell.

There are not many people at the bus stop but no vacant spaces on the bench. Two older women and a girl are seated on it. Had they been Nigerian, their broad hips would not have taken up so much space. He stands by a streetlamp and waits. In the short time he has arrived in Braamfontein, the bus system is one of the first things he was acquainted with. The bus home will arrive soon.

If he had stayed at the restaurant any longer, he would have missed the final bus and had to have walked home in the dark, which was not safe in a neighbourhood like this. He had holed up in the neighbourhood for lack of funds. His money had been wiped out at the airport, most of it when he had to bribe the immigration officer. He hoped that with his first paycheque at the restaurant, he could get himself a more agreeable accommodation in a safer neighbourhood.

He reaches for his phone, to idle away the time and keep his eyes from straying to the broad hips and full bosom of a woman who just arrived at the bus stop. There is nothing new on his phone to hold his attention. No new messages. None from the young man, Chike.

The bus arrives and pulls up at the bus stop. Thankful, Osas pockets his phone and files in with the other passengers. He pays his fare, heads for the lonely tail end the bus, settles by into a window seat, and looks out as the bus pulls away from the stop, joining the evening traffic.

His mind wanders. How easily can one begin to settle in a place that initially struck them as strange and hostile? How many weeks has it been since he came to this place? South Africa had made an impression on him the moment he had landed, not something he can forget quickly.

He had touched down at the O.R. Tambo International Airport at noon and waited at Passport Check. The immigration officer had looked at his passport, then at him, repeatedly. "Come with me," the officer had said, stepping out of the glass-partitioned cubicle and signalling for a colleague to take his place. Osas did not know where he got the strength from, but he was somehow able to follow the officer, who seemed to be labouring to carry his bulk around. The officer led a frightened Osas into a small room.

"What are you intending to come into the country for?" he asked as soon as he shut the door.

"Tourism," Osas managed to let out.

The officer nodded knowingly. A weak smile played at the corners of his mouth. He fetched some surgical gloves from a drawer and put them on. Terrified, Osas knew not what to think anymore.

"Officer is there a problem?" he asked. The quiver in his voice betraying him.

"Do you have anything in your pockets?"

"Yes."

"Please bring them all out and place them on the desk there," he instructed, gesturing at a white desk that claimed much of the room.

Osas obeyed. He got out his phone and placed it on the table. He unslung his satchel and put it on the table as well.

"Is that all?"

"Yes, sir."

"Good. Spread out your arms. And your legs too."

Osas obeyed. The immigration officer frisked him, taking his time to feel around his crotch.

"Do you have any drugs or illicit substances in your possession?"

"No,

"This is yours, right?" he asked, pointing at the satchel on the desk.

"Yes, sir. It is my bag."

The officer reached for the satchel, opened it and upturned its contents onto the table. He felt around the satchel for any hidden pockets. There was none. He picked up the Yellow Fever Card and examined it.

"This Yellow Fever Card is fake."

"Sir?"

"You heard me right."

Osas's bones felt like gel. He had paid one thousand naira for the Yellow Fever Card at the airport in Lagos. Some woman in a nurse's uniform had simply filled in his details and passport number into the card, signed, stamped and handed him the card. She never gave him any shots.

"We can't let you into the country."

"But sir, please ..."

"Hold on, my friend, but for $100, we will forget about your Yellow Fever Card."

Osas had only $150 in his pocket. He handed the officer a $100 bill. The man pocketed it and became jovial that instant. He helped Osas put his things back into his satchel, and then led him out.

As Osas waited for a taxi, another man drew up next to him. He was waiting for a taxi too. Approaching middle age, he wore neatly tailored chinos and blazer suit. It was obvious that he was East African, perhaps Kenyan, and well-to-do.

A taxi swerved into the curb. The driver came around. He haggled briefly him, then helped the man put his luggage into the trunk. The Kenyan would have settled into the backseat, but the driver talked him into getting into the front-seat instead.

The taxi took unnecessarily long to leave. The Kenyan stumbled out of the taxi, and the car zoomed off immediately. The Kenyan began to shout and cry. He threw his hands in the air. It was then that Osas realised that the driver had robbed the man of his wallet, jewellery and blazer. His luggage was gone too.

Osas exhales.

South Africa had created a fearful first impression. However, what has he not seen in this life? He is steadily settling in. Surely, he will make it here. South Africa has to favour him; at all costs. It will be a matter of time. Just a short wait, he hopes.

Osas' eyes spring wide open. He lies still, recollecting his thoughts. He has had a bad dream. A very bad one. It had been about Papi. In the dream, unrecognisable people shot Papi, and his corpse was been dragged around the streets.

He turns in the bed. April is sleeping next to him, her light snores rising and falling in a rhythmic pattern. The small sharp curve of her hips stand out against the loose-fitting boxer shorts he had worn after bathing a few hours ago. Chike has not come back for three nights straight, and so he had allowed

April to come over just a couple of hours after midnight.

He sits up. The room feels hot and airless. Getting off the bed, he heads for the window, slides the glass and leaves the curtains parted. The clock on the wall says six in the morning, but outside it looks much earlier. The bed creaks as April turns in her sleep. He waits for her snoring to resume, but it does not.

"Why you no dey sleep?"She asks groggily.

He glances at her and then turns his attention to the streets.

"I no fit sleep."

The bed creaks more as she sits up. "I hope say everything dey okay?"

"Na just bad dream."

"Wetin happen for the dream?"

"They kill Papi."

April falls silent. He can guess the news is shocking to her. Of course, it has to be. They both understand that Papi is a stabilising force within the Nigerian and African underworld community. If ever he is to go down violently, his sudden absence would create a gaping vacuum. There would be a fierce contest for territory. It would turn bloody and stay that way until stability returned. Even Madam

Ruth would be affected, and her girls, too. As long as Papi still waxes strong, her business and influence are secured.

"This one wey you dey dream this dream. Na wa o. Abeg we never get ourself after the one wey do Arnold."

"True. Arnold matter shock me, I swear. Na since I hear about the way them take kill that man I begin to dey get bad dream about Papi."

"God no go gree. Papi no be ordinary man like Arnold."

Osas agrees.

Papi is not like Arnold in so many ways. The Tanzanian was a legitimate businessman until his gruesome murder. They say he had come to South Africa many years ago, a poor boy from a small rural town with all of his worldly possessions packed into a woven bag, which he always held pressed against his chest. According to the stories, he could barely speak or understand anything that was not Swahili.

Ten years passed, and he made millions from importing sugar. But it did not end with sugar. There were rumours that he had his sights set on the mines. News circulated that he planned to set up a bank with the intent to support the Tanzanian business community in South Africa. This idea got some locals riled up. He was always in the news; always on people's lips. It had struck everyone when the news came that multiple bullets had struck down Arnold, including one to his head. It had been a drive-by. He had just dropped his kid off at school, kissed him goodbye. People said his killers must have mistaken him for someone else. No one knew the truth. Arnold was dead and that settled it. There had been two other victims of the drive-by, but only his death was acknowledged. In death as in life, Arnold's shadow loomed over people.

"God no go shame us," April says.

"Yes."

"No worry. Nothing go do Papi."

Osas nods and walks to the bed. He sits down. April wraps her arms around his naked body and kisses his neck. It sends a tingle to his groin. He returns the kiss on her lips, allowing her to guide him back to the bed. Their kissing turns passionate, as she mounts him and peels off his oversized shirt that she wears.

When Osas thinks about April, he thinks about her as that woman who loves Oprah Winfrey so much.

April sees so much of Oprah in herself. The icon had had a tough life as a young girl. It is same with her too. Life had been tough and bleak. There were times when she considered suicide as a way out of it all but then she had come into contact with Oprah, and she had seen hope. There was now something to live for, to look forward to and hope for. They said Oprah is the most influential black woman in America, and the world. She would have to be a goddess, then. Of course, she is, because only a goddess would have given such hope and zeal to live as Oprah gives her. The celebrity has practically thrown light into her darkened world, and things no longer look as bleak as they did. She never misses any opportunity to watch Oprah on TV or to follow up on any of her Instagram updates. It never matters that Oprah never reacted to her comments on her social media posts. It does not matter. It would be too much to ask for. Seeing her talk and do her thing was enlightening enough for her, and so when the news came that Oprah is coming to South Africa, April practically goes berserk.

The other girls are not usually interested in her thrill for Oprah, and so she did not bother them with the news of Oprah's visit.

But they sense that something is amiss.

They talk lightly about how April seems very excited and goes about her day in high spirits. She never picks offence at anything, and she is very cheerful. The girls make jests insinuating that she must have gotten a new client who may be intent on paying off her debts to Madam Ruth and keeping her for himself. She laughs at these talks but does nothing to verify or debunk them. The girls let her be. Life on the streets has so many distractions, enough to discourage a lavishing of too much attention on any one thing.

April asks Osas questions about Oprah's visit. Anyone who looks remotely capable of supplying her with the information she needs, she approaches.

That is how she meets Vusi.

It was in a club she meets the man. He is a big man seated by himself at a table, sipping a glass of sparkling wine and seemingly soaking in every element of his environment. His leather jacket stands out amongst every article of his clothing. Someone had hinted to April that the man was a show promoter and had a foot in almost every show and public event that was being planned in Johannesburg.

April had gone to meet him, and she had worn her best charm while at it, and he had softened up towards her almost immediately.

"I hear that Oprah is coming to town," she broaches the matter immediately they had exchanged pleasantries, and he had told her his name and confirmed that he was into show biz.

"Oprah? You mean Oprah Winfrey?"

"Yes. They say she is visiting her school on the eighteenth."

He had nodded while taking a sip of his drink.

"I want to see her, please. Can you do that for me?"

He regards her in silence. The dancing lights of the club do not afford her a chance to study his countenance and perhaps read into them. She thinks she notices him lick his lips. If she had been naïve, she would have thought he was licking off the taste of his wine on his lips, but it was not the case. It was more than that.

"Let's go somewhere quiet, somewhere we can talk."

"Where?"

"My car. It's parked outside."

He downs the last of his drink and ushers her out of the club. The street feels cold and quite lonely, except for a few people hanging outside and drinking. A couple kiss at a corner where the streetlights did not give away too much. The girl slaps the man's hands away when he reaches for her breasts. Despite her exposed hands, shoulders and legs, April resists the urge to hug herself against the cold windy night.

April and Vusi arrive at his car. It is a Chevrolet that had seen better times. Its state of degradation is made more pronounced considering that it is sandwiched between a Mercedes and a Ford SUV in the parking lot.

"Let's get in and talk," he says as he holds the front passenger door open for her. He shuts the door gently after her and then goes around to help himself in. "What were you saying back there," he says as he settles his bulk in the driver seat. She is able to study his face better in the semi-darkness of the car. He looks older than he had appeared back in the club and he would look much better without the earring that looked like it was pressed into a ball of chewed bubble gum instead of an ear lobe.

"I want you to arrange for me to meet with Oprah, even if it's for a few minutes."

"You know how difficult this is. It is not part of the schedule we have on her program."

"I know, but I believe you can make it happen," April says, beginning to sound desperate.

Vusi lets out a sigh. "Anyway, I never said it can't be done." April's face lightens up. "But what's in it for me?"

Of course, she had been foolish to think anyone

cared about granting her wishes for nothing. "How much?"

"A piece of you."

"Sex?"

"Yes. I take you to my place. You fuck me real good now, and then you repeat the same when the job is done."

April cringed. "I thought it is money you need."

"No. You will not be able to pay for it if I should spell out my price. I have discounted it down to something you can easily afford."

April regards the man with heightened apprehension. She understands the unspoken codes of the streets, especially where it concerns rendering sexual services. No one does so free. Osas is an exception, and of course, giving sexual favours in exchange for finally getting to meet Oprah in person is not too high a price to pay. She could give an arm if it came to that, but something told her that Vusi is not to be trusted. There is a very high possibility that he has no connections with the event planning in question. She could not shake off this feeling. Listening to such feeling had kept her safe on the streets and the job for this long, and she was not going to begin to disobey it. Surely not now.

"So what do you say?" he asks.

"We will meet some other time."

"If you are not okay with the idea of going with me to my house we could do it right here, in my car."

"It will have to be some other time."

"Okay a blowjob."

April bolts out of the car before the man could begin to entertain any idea of getting physical. It always turns out that way if one is not decisive enough. Stupid! She curses as she makes her way back into the club even as she imagines how little the man's penis would be with all the bulk and buttocks he had on him.

BIG CITY

Everyone knows Papi is a dangerous man. They say he could give the chills to the devil. He is intelligent and lacks inhibitions, and for this reason, his friends stay wary and his foes respectful. Whenever the occasion presents itself, he exceeds his reputation for violence and appears never to lose any sleep over it. Those know his story well blame his current behaviour on his rough childhood. Children in his rural community always laughed at his flabby tummy. They would call him "Christmas balloon." In school, at football games during the recess, Papi would not be chosen because the other boys thought he could not move his plump body. They said he could not tackle or strike the ball. No team wanted him. It made for a merrier laugh the more Papi begged or cried. Most often, he went to a quiet corner to sob. He began to dread school. Many times, he feigned sickness so that his parents would let him stay at home.

One evening, on his way home from a grocery store, a lanky boy with a long neck stopped him along a snaky bush pathway, demanding that he hand over everything he had purchased. Papi stood there, fixed to the ground. The boy snatched the nylon shopping bag from him and Papi, unable to believe what had just happened, stood dumbstruck as the thief took off. The rage that Papi had kept locked deep inside for so long burst to the surface. He followed the thief in hot pursuit and just when he was beginning to think he would never catch up, the thief's legs knocked together, sending him crashing to the ground. Papi snatched a log of wood lying on the ground nearby and smashed it upon the thief in full force. The thief began to cry and plead. It was like nothing Papi had experienced before. For the first time, he felt some sense of accomplishment. He did not listen to the boy's pleas but brought the wood hard on the thief's temple. The thief became still. Papi did not stop. He hit and hit until the body was no longer recognisable. This was Papi's first murder.

Papi relieved that moment for days. It pleased him so much that he soon went on a rampage.

Everyone who had ever taunted or shamed him was ambushed and knocked out before they had a chance to react. Some survived the attacks. Others did not. People grew wary of him, many wondering if he was behind the many unexplained murders in the town. Others would not entertain the idea. They could not conceive the possibility that a mere boy was capable of such gruesome acts of violence.

Soon, Papi caught the attention of a local gang. They recruited and trained him, and he learned fast. Violence came naturally to him and so, over the years, he rose through the ranks and turned into a force on the streets. Politicians contracted him for assassination jobs. Not once did he fail, and he had a rule of never allowing himself to be anyone's pawn, especially when it was a person of influence. He gave only as much loyalty as the job demanded. Once a job was done, he was available to take any new contract even when it demanded that he put a bullet into the head of the previous client. He was a weapon, open to anyone who could afford his services. His reputation spread. The ruling class said he knew too much. He was both poison and gold– valuable when he worked for you, dangerous against you.

Papi got into serious trouble only once when the military declared him wanted for arranging the killing of four officers who had congregated at a local bar early one night. Word got out to Papi. The heat was intense. His powerful clients could no longer be relied on. Fearing for his life, Papi snuck out of the country and escaped to South Africa.

So much time has passed. Papi is now burlier, more imposing. His temper has worsened. His reputation followed him to South Africa. The mere prospect of having a conversation with Papi seemed dreadful to many. He ran a Nigerian cartel in South Africa whose reach spread across the continent, Europe, and America. His nightclub thrived, but it was a front.

Papi now sits behind a vintage mahogany desk, barking orders into the phone. The veins stand out on his neck, and his forehead glistens with sweat. The person on the other end of the line has every reason to sound jittery.

"I dey warn you, Philip," Papi growls, banging a monstrous clenched fist with bejewelled fingers on the vintage Mahogany desk. "No play games with me. Remit my forty thousand rands by Monday! Or I go come find you for Cape Town."

He listens to the person on the other end for a moment. "You know say I no dey talk wetin I no fit do! You want try me *abi*? Guy, if you do anyhow, you go see anyhow!"

Ending the call, he throws the phone on the desk, cursing, breathing harder. Just then, the buzzer for the outer security gate of the club sounds. In his usual paranoia, Papi stares into the video monitor beside his desk. The two men asking to be let in are not foes. He lets them in and watches them walk up the passage towards his office. As they come to the second security gate, he lets them in again with the press of a button.

The one to first step in is Chike. His tattooed arms and dreadlocks lend some edge to his heavy build and handsome features. Close on his heels waits an unsmiling teenager with an Afro-styled haircut and darting beady eyes that seem capable of seeing beyond the walls of the room.

"Chike," Papi grunts, leaning back into his big office chair. "Na you dey look like you bring police with you so?"

"I'm sorry, Don Papi," Chike says. "Good afternoon, boss."

Papi snorts, as though impatient for the visitors to leave now that they have disturbed his peace. "Wetin make you waste time? You suppose don come back since two-thirty."

"Don Papi, the guy no call me on time," Chike explains. "I just get to wait."

Papi stares at him with an expression so cold that Chike is forced to lower his gaze to the floor. Papi now turns his full attention to the teenager. "Wetin be your name?"

"Osas, sir," the boy replies. Papi is surprised by the boy's voice. It seems to him to have a strange quality to it, though he cannot say what it is exactly.

Papi stares at the new Nigerian recruit; there is something inexplicable about him, a feeling not easy to capture in words. "My name na Don Papi," he says, reclining back in his leather chair.

"Yes, sir?"

"Boss!" Papi reacts suddenly, surprising the boy but not Chike, who by now is used to Papi's volatile behaviour. "You call me boss."

"Yes boss," Osas says slowly, as though weighing the word on his tongue.

"Good," Papi says, nodding. "Why you delay?"

Osas swallows hard, anxiety now evident in his voice. "De reverend sisters for de camp no gree me comot before de induction finish. And I no been quick see person to thief phone from."

Papi lifts his bulk from his chair. He walks around to the front of the large desk, half-sitting on its edge.

"Who tell you to steal phone?" he asks, fixing his gaze hard on Osas. "If you been ask anybody nicely, them for borrow you phone."

Osas opens his mouth to speak, but nothing comes out. Papi can see the fear and concern in his face.

"Where the phone?" Papi demands.

Osas hastily fetches in his pocket for phone. Chike snatches it from him and reverently hands it to Papi. Both Chike and Osas are startled when the big man lets the phone drop to the floor before stomping it repeatedly to pieces.

When Papi is finished smashing the device, he straightens then says casually, "No be Naija be this." His manner takes on a casual air, as though nothing awkward has just happened. "You gats dey very smart. Smart, sharp and fast." He stares Osas in the eye and then holds out an open palm. "Your passport."

Osas produces the document from his hip pocket and hands it over to Papi.

"You go get am back when you finish to pay me my fifteen thousand rands complete," Papi informs him matter-of-factly, tossing the passport onto the desk.

"But boss them been say na five thousand rands I go balance you," Osas states, wide-eyed with exasperation.

"Other expenses dey wey them no tell you. Abi you no go sleep for house?" Papi turns to Chike. "You don show am the place?"

"Aside from KY barbershop where I stop sell market, na only room I carry am go to drop bag," Chike answers.

Papi seats himself behind his desk. "Take am around the turf, then bring am back for night."

"Yes, boss."

Papi opens his lower desk drawer and takes out a small packet. He tosses it casually at Osas to catch. "Them don already tie am one-one gram. Na thirty grams dey there. Make we see wetin you fit do."

He waves at them dismissively as his phone begins to ring.

As they stroll along the old train station in Braamfontein, which connects the city to Durban, Osas cannot stop thinking that he is about to fulfil his dreams. He is not aware of the South African pedestrians who walk by; the kind who usually ignores people like him or mumbles something incomprehensible under their breath that often includes the word *kwerekwere*.

For someone who had grown up in the deadliest parts of Benin-City, this place, free of death, was a paradise. For many years, he had lived with his grandmother, who sold bales of cloth at a roadside shed at Holy Cross, New Benin. He had no memory of his mother because she had left home when he was still a toddler. And he had never known who his father was since there were no pictures of him anywhere in the small flat that always smelt of crayfish and rotting rats. His grandmother was much too secretive to explain his birth.

Nothing Osas did pleased her. The floor was poorly swept, the louvres not clean enough. Couldn't he see the oil stains on the plates? In the old woman's eyes, he was a failure. It was no surprise that Osas proved her right by not lasting long in school. He got into fights that left him bruised and, what's more, every time his classmates misplaced something, it would always be found in his school bag. At the age of fifteen, Osas was finally expelled for stealing a teacher's purse. He did not tell his grandmother about any of this; the woman did not care much about his activities, anyways. Each morning, he would put on his school uniform and head to Uselu market, where he soon became friends with a bus driver plying the Ugbowo axis. The man took him on as the conductor. Osas never forgot the first night he was paid for his services. He knew boys that spent money on whores and at nightclubs. But these were not his thing. He kept the money hidden in a box that he buried in the garden at home. He began to save and dream of the day he would move out of that stinking apartment, creep from under the shadows of the indifferent old woman and make something of himself.

A handful of years later on the bus, he heard a passenger with dark glasses say to his friend, "That guy dey Rome as I dey follow you talk so. Na me run de package for am."

"You mean say Ivie no dey Benin again?"

"Go him Facebook go check am na."

Incredulity flickered on the other man's face. "You don mean it?"

Osas had heard of agents who worked out travel passages for those seeking to leave the country in search of better lives. It had been his impression that those highly influential people kept their connections secret. Nobody indulging in illegal migration went around boasting like this fellow on the bus. There was an air of assurance about him, the look of someone capable of changing your life with a single phone call.

"Give me your number, make we reason later," the other passenger said.

Staring out the window at the flitting landscape, the whipping wind making his eyes moist, Osas memorised the phone number of this unusual travel agent as he spoke out the digits to his neighbour. Osas knew this was an important moment for him because this man had the power to change his life.

A week later, just as he had sat down to eat, Osas' grandmother approached him on the veranda, contempt etched on her face.

"Who be that girl wey I see you with for junction?"

The aggression in her tone provoked him.

"What girl?" he snapped.

"No, ask me yeye question this night. I say, na who be the girl wey you been dey hold anyhow for the public?"

Osas didn't know that she had seen him and Oghogho, the most beautiful girl in all the world, the girl with the large searching eyes, perfectly shaped lips, flawless skin and tantalising breasts. She lived many streets away and always took the trouble to come see him in his part of town. She would bring her fine art assignments that she urgently needed help with because she was terrible at drawing. Osas was a skilled artist, natural with line, form, and colouration, and who, given the choice, had the prospect of being a modest success if he ever thought of opening a studio.

They would meet at his house while his grandmother sold her bales at Holy Cross. They would sit on the floor in the sunlight, his arm sometimes touching hers, and he would try to show her what he was doing with her pictures. They laughed often. She had told him of her life in a house full of siblings and the dreams she had for herself. In return, Osas told her of the horrors of living with a grandmother who did not love him, how he had no mother or father.

They had shared their stories, but Osas wanted to share much more with Oghogho. Yet, with each of his advances, she would just giggle, and call him a silly boy. They had kissed the last time. She had even let Osas touch her breast before softly pushing him away and pleading that he stop. Osas had needed all his willpower to stop. However, he knew he loved her and would do absolutely anything she asked of him.

When at long last, she had answered his messages since that day, she asked to meet him somewhere they had never met before. Osas had arrived an hour earlier at the junction, filled with hope, believing they would make their love for one another public. He would ask her father for her hand. He imagined marrying her and was thinking of the speech he would give of the life he would build for the two of them when he saw her coming towards him through the crowds. The reluctance with which she came and the look of pain on her face made his heart sink.

He asked her what was wrong, thinking something had happened to her family.

She was silent for a few moments, and then asked him to hug her. He held her for as long as she would let him, and then she began to cry. Through her tears, she told him she was pregnant. Without giving him a chance to respond, she pulled away and ran. Osas knew he would never see her again and that her running through the crowd was the last time he would ever see her.

Osas had never walked so far or for so long in his life. When he finally found his way home, he threw himself on his bed and passed out in exhaustion. The next day he lay crying until, eventually, hunger forced him into the kitchen.

He realised now that his grandmother had seen him and Oghogho.

"Osas, no be you I dey follow talk?"

"Na person wey I dey do assignment for," he said.

"Person wey you dey do assignment for? See your life for outside. You dey do assignment for people wey dey go school but see you na. You don burn your school uniform. People wey get enough sense dey classroom dey learn, you dey waka for night dey look for who you go draw wetin I no know for."

"No be so—"

"No dey follow me talk," she snapped. "See, make I tell you. If you no start to dey bring money for this house, I go pursue you comot. You hear me so? If you want useless like your mama and papa, no be for my house."

Osas stared at her for a long time and the old woman glared back, unblinking. He pushed his meal aside, straightened, and walked out of the house into the garden.

Nothing changed for Osas. Every day was the same, with his grandmother always there to remind him that life is far from perfect, that one should not bask for too long in any momentary succour. In that setting filled with misery and a sense of his inferiority, Osas espoused an activity that gradually brought him admiration. He drew and painted. Some acquaintances saw his work and told others.

People began to ask him to draw and paint portraits of them.

The bus driver who Osas had worked for as a conductor became a friend. He let Osas use his room as a studio while he was out buying and selling. Fame accompanied the upsurge of sexual encounters. Osas realised his models held him in fascination. To them, he was like a spirit whose magical skill with pencil and brush would immortalise them. Osas had acquired a glossy foreign book of nude portraits, left on the bus by a passenger. His models leafed through the illustrated book, completely absorbed. He urged one of them to take off her blouse.

"I have to see the whole person... that's how a great artist works. Oyibo people understand this. You see the paintings in that book?" he asked.

The young woman, obviously keen to identify with foreign sophisticates, slipped off her blouse, and later, her skirt and underwear. The other models followed suit.

Osas' voyeuristic delight in seeing those primly covered bodies naked was exploded.

He would urge a model to turn a certain way so that his gaze could rake her breasts and nipples, the pubic hair, and the rippling thighs, while his erection almost split his khaki shorts. Some of the sessions ended in sex. Osas' adolescent hormonal cravings finally received sumptuous gratification.

Onaiwu, the owner of the room, sometimes walked in on a nude painting session. The naked female would squirm and in panic grab her pants and bra. "No worry, it's okay," Osas would assure her. "Na my brother now. Na him get this room."

After persistent cajoling, Onaiwu, too, succeeded in fucking two of the girls. Apart from models, some callers were simply curious or idle. They sat on the wooden bench on the veranda outside Onaiwu's room. From them, Osas heard tales of an idyllic world abroad. "Mehn, my sister Irenonse cross over to Italy. No be small money she dey send now. Her money na'im dey keep our family going."

"Abroad," yearned another, "overseas! The naira is nothing now. Abroad, you just make cash.

Hard currency. They say no light wahala, no water wahala, everything dey, and all those oyibo girls... Even Odia who no be anything here, just one kind yahoo boy, he go America... I dey see am for Facebook. Mehn, the guy is living big. When we talk on phone, the way he dey sound, just like Obama when he be President. Once you go overseas, you are made."

The more fantastic stories of foreign lands he heard, the more he began to dream of those far realms. He believed he could amass wealth and attain fame if he managed to leave Nigeria. His present situation caged him like a cell. Once outside Nigeria, he would spring and soar into his true form. "Leave Naija, leave Naija," his heart kept urging. "You miss your destiny by staying in Nigeria." Like Osas would say, "If the snake bites the tortoise, he breaks off his mouth."

One day he could take it no more. He retrieved his safe box from his secret hole in the garden that had been covered with a thin board and sand. He took out all the money he had saved up, counted it quickly, and then took out his phone and dialled the number he had committed to memory. Someone answered after only two rings.

"Hello," the agent said.

"Good evening, sir," Osas began. "I need your help."

He sat in the unusual travel agent's lightly furnished sitting room the next day. The man introduced himself as Damilare and presented Osas with the list of available countries he thought he could migrate to without breaking his bank. "The cheapest na Italy, but na through desert that one be. You fit walk?"

Osas had heard the awful stories of what befell many of the people who had marched across the Sahara on their way to Europe. He felt that would be a fitting end to his dreams.

"Which other country you fit help with?" he asked.

"Well, Ghana and Rwanda still dey," he said. "And I still get for South Africa, but I go yarn you as the matter be. All these places, especially South Africa, na bar my connection them dey push for there. If you reach there, my connect go give you accommodation, but you gats work hard. Like, hard."

Osas nodded. His life was already hard.

"So which country you want make I run for you?" Damilare stared intently.

Osas glanced at the crumpled piece of paper in the man's hand. He had suffered enough. Fleeing from the humiliation his grandmother always meted out to him and Oghogho's betrayal was all that Osas could think of. He had to leave. It was time to become a man, pull his way through life. Ghana was too close to home, and many people were going there already. He did not want to go to a place where someone might know him. All he knew about Rwanda was that some popular film had been made about the country's civil war. He did not want to go to a war-torn country. The march to Italy would be a crawl through the hottest part of hell.

But in South Africa, he would be hooked up with someone and have a roof over his head. He had heard that life in South Africa for Nigerians could be lucrative. He could make a lot of money there.

"SA," he said. "I want South Africa."

Damilare smiled. He had known the boy would make this choice. That was how Osas came to be walking down a street whose name he did not know how to pronounce.

It felt like a dream when he got his visa. His sensations on the flight were indescribable. South Africa, he thought, SA. It was his first time on a plane, and he was both thrilled and terrified as it took off. He looked around, and other passengers, obviously used to flying, seemed unmoved by the experience. Elation followed him into the clouds. He was above the rest of humanity; he felt scornful of all he had left behind in Benin.

In Benin, the elders would say that when the soft mud that makes up a house cave in, the sand used to build it, washes away into gaping holes. That was why apprehension briefly punctured Osas' growing elation.

He was going to an unknown place.

What would he find there? He had heard of South Africa described as a 20th-century miracle, a place where black people had been treated like scum for decades and had now become the black man's paradise. Osas began to regain his optimism. He had heard that many Nigerians, considered failures at home, were making fortunes in South Africa. His heart was aglow. Tears of joy began to slide down his face.

The journey to South Africa felt so long ago now. He had already been in Braamfontein for a while, had met the big boss. His sole focus now revolved around making more cash. Chike tapped him on the back, jolting him out of his reverie.

"Nna, since morning na just look you dey look."

Osas stares at him. The silence seems to irritate Chike.

"You no dey talk, abi you no hear wetin I talk?" Chike says. Without waiting for Osas's response, he continues and points to a booth in the distance. "Follow my hand. Na there them dey sell ticket. You fit connect anywhere from this station—"

Just then, there is a commotion ahead, among a

group of aggressively chattering men. In their midst is a young man close to tears, an obvious prey for a ruthless local gang.

"You stay here," Chike orders Osas and starts for the street corner. As he approaches, with his fists clenched, he sees the young man, fair-skinned and not South African, probably in his early twenties. A gangster grips him by the throat and holds a glinting blade to his Adam's apple. While the young man is pinned to the wall, another gangster unclasps his watch and steals his wallet.

"You fuck boys!" Chike snarls, charging at them like an offended bull.

Seeing Chike, the gang disperses in different directions similar to the seeds of a burst oil bean.

"Idiots!" Chike curses after them then turns to the stranger who has dropped from the wall and is now on all fours. "You okay, brother?"

The boy nods, visibly shaken and struggling to control his breath. He is soaked in sweat. "They got my watch and wallet."

"Well, they don't get your life too," Chike says, helping him to his feet. "Sorry man. Those clowns make a point of targeting other Africans. Once they see a pink man, their balls shrink. Spineless cunts, all of dem. Osas!" Chike calls. Hearing no response, he turns around, but he is not there any longer. He grinds his teeth in annoyance.

"Looking for somebody?" the man asks.

"My boy, now he is gone."

"So, what will you do now?"

"I'll find him," Chike says. "Let's get you a cup of tea first."

The man stares at him with incredulity.

"Just one African courtesy to another."

"I'm not from Africa."

Chike's brows crinkle. "Oh. Where are you from?"

"I was born in Canada, but my father ran off with a Canadian woman. My mom and I returned to Zimbabwe after that."

Chike looks at him sternly, because he knows he is lying. Chike always says that people in Southern Africa lie a lot. That it was the reason why they are always criticising people who lie better than they do. Or whom they think is smarter. He will also think to himself, as an Igbo man, that the corpse does not know that maggots have eaten it. He looked at the young liar again and shook his head. *Born in Canada, my Naija ass*, he said, inaudibly.

"Interesting. You new here. I'm Chike."

The boy wipes his mouth. "Chamai."

Chike smiles. "I have this feeling we gon be good friends."

The string that holds the parcel: if the string becomes untied, the parcel opens.

Osas is getting good at what he does. From where he stands in the shadows, a foreign face in a sea of people, Osas watches an impressively dressed pink man. The man stands out so much in his expensive suit that Osas cannot help but smile. The man carelessly carries a briefcase in one hand and some files in the other. He exits the train station. Osas forces himself to wait for a few seconds and then follows, stalking his prey. He knows this is going to be an easy catch.

For Osas, he believes that pink people are not smart. Especially pink South Africans. He would say, "Those ones that call themselves Afrikaner." Most times, when the Nigerians gather in bars or barbing salons, or even in the restaurants, they spend time, discussing South Africans. Once, Osas would remember this that a Nigerian said that South Africans are very unreliable people and talk a lot.

"They say things they can't do!" one said, with a slight Yoruba accent. "These people can lie also."

A young Cameroonian woman, a hairstylist, chipped in: "If you invite a South African to an event, he will say he will come. On the day of the event, you will not see him, and he will not apologise at all."

Another voice agreed in French.

"I can tell you that they are very dishonest," one other voice added, obviously, with a French tilt. "They have no dignity."

"Abeg," Osas said, "we can't be criticising our hosts. If we do not like their snaky ways, we can go back to our countries."

Then, a brassy voice added, "South Africans hate honesty. They cannot stand it. They will begin to cry. So, no need to say it. They are fraudulent people!"

So, back to Osas and the pink man.

As the pink man turns a corner, Osas snatches a newspaper from a distracted roadside vendor's pile. He is enjoying himself. He feels invincible. He quickens his pace. He aims to overtake the unsuspecting pink man. Once he is ahead of the man, he pretends to be engrossed in the paper and turns abruptly, bumping into the man and knocking his briefcase and papers to the ground.

"Eh—," the man exclaims, the foreign accent unmistakable.

"Sorry, shit, sorry!" Osas acts equally surprised.

The man looks Osas in the eye and then mutters something under his breath before bending down to pick up his things.

"Sorry, sir. Let me help you," Osas offers, placing one hand heavily on his shoulder and another gently on his wrist.

"It's fine. Just leave me alone," the man says, snatching the briefcase closer to himself and gathering the scattered documents from the pavement.

Osas apologises once more and steps back. "Go, no problema"

The stranger straightens and continues on his way. A few minutes later, he fleetingly glances at his wrist and stiffens. There is no watch. He swirls round in panic but it is pointless. Coming from Italy, he should know better. Or could it be that the African *Mafioso* is weirder than the Italian is?

Entering a shopping centre, Osas straps the timepiece to his wrist. He rubs the watch's glass with his shirtsleeves and smiles. A Tag Heuer. He goes into Edgar's shop, ignoring the security guard who stares at him with more than a disinterested glance before disappearing down an aisle. Osas has not reached the end of the aisle when he senses someone trailing him from a distance. It makes him wary but he chooses to smile. Playing hide and seek makes the game fun. The fly that follows meat does not starve. He will outwit the security guard who thinks Osas does not know when he is being monitored. The man is as stupid as the uniform he is wearing.

Osas stops at a glass case with many glittering watches on display. He looks at the price tags, comparing them. The security guard materialises.

"Can we help you?" the guard asks, not even trying to hide his distaste.

A woman walking past says something to the guard in Sotho and they both laugh.

"I let you know when I do," Osas says, trying to act nonchalant.

The guard's gaze rests on the watch on Osas' wrist. Osas is unnerved; he needs to get out of the shop if he is to avoid any trouble. Calmly, he strolls to another row, where he picks up a pair of socks, and then heads for the till.

The security guard hovers. "Excuse me, sir?" he walks towards Osas.

Osas pretends not to hear, knowing he must act fast. Thoughts of being led away in handcuffs rattle him. His mind races. He considers putting the watch under a toy on a nearby shelf, but then, the handbag on the shoulder of the woman in front of him catches his attention. The zipper is open all the way. As she steps up to make her payment, Osas stows the wristwatch into her handbag. At that same time, he feels a rough hand grip his shoulder.

"Please step back, sir."

Without a squeak of protest, Osas obeys. The woman is still busy with her payment. She will leave soon. Osas knows he has to finish with the security guard as quickly as he can.

"Let me see your hands," the guard orders him.

Osas holds out his hands to the security guard who pushes up his sleeves. The guard is visibly perplexed. He pats Osas down and checks his pockets. Osas does not take his eyes off the woman with the handbag as she heads towards the exit.

The guard straightens and stares Osas in the eye. "*Wena*! You foreigners must leave now. We do not want you here anymore."

"This must be a mistake," Osas says, looking around casually but noting the direction the woman turns.

The guard considers what to do. He seems to be at a loss for a moment, and then heads off. Osas tosses the socks and marches out of the store, feigning indignation.

There is a mild wind outside the shopping centre. The road is busy. Osas looks around to his left and right but does not see the woman. He makes a quick choice and scurries down the street when, suddenly, to his relief, he spots her strolling past a KFC outlet on the other side of the road. He dashes across, almost stepping in front of a mini-bus taxi. The driver presses down on his horn, swearing loudly. Osas ignores him, races past the other pedestrians, and then grabs the woman by the arm just as she is about to walk into a gym.

"Hey, wait!"

The woman spins around, terror all over her face. Osas' heart plummets. *This is not the woman*, he realises. She does not have a white handbag.

"Don't fucking touch me, you cockroach." The woman pulls her arm free and storms into the gym.

Osas groans. All that hard work as though it was for nothing. It makes him angry. He blames it on the stupid security guard. Hearing a chuckle behind him, Osas turns around to find a tall, well-built man watching him. The man is mixed race and has hazel eyes.

"Ain't that a bummer, mate? Happened to me

before," he says, wiping sweat from his forehead. He extends a hand to Osas. "Andre. And what's your name?"

"Osas. You fit call me Oscar."

"Interesting," Andre remarks. "Nice to meet you, Osas."

Osas stares at him. Andre chuckles.

"I get that look all the time. My mom is from England, but my old man is a homeboy," he says. "I'm a model but I also work here. It's an excuse to work out for free," Andre laughs. "And you don't need to tell me, I already know, you're Nigerian."

Osas warms immediately to this friendly man. "How you know?"

"You think I no sabi Nigerian pidgin?" Andre says, startling Osas. "I've been to Nigeria twice, and I loved the place." Andre leans in closer, conspiratorially, and whispers, "Especially the shorties!" His laughter is infectious and Osas joins him. "Got somewhere to be?" he asks when the laughter has died down.

Osas thinks of the lost watch and shrugs. He knows he should try to make up for the loss by finding other pockets to pick, but he likes this man.

"You look like someone who could help me out," Andre says, wrapping his muscled arm around

Osas' shoulder. "I'll pick up my stuff and we'll find somewhere to talk, yeah?"

"Yeah," Osas agrees.

"Correct guy! I will be back in a minute. Please wait over there," he directs Osas, pointing to a sitting area inside the gym.

Osas settles himself down uncomfortably. He is not used to gyms, and it makes him feel weak. He is suddenly reminded of Oghogho. He tries to concentrate on the matter at hand. He needs to make as much money as he can. That stupid security guard has cost him at least a few hundred. Osas decides the security guard should pay for the loss. What about this man, Osas wonders. What does this man want from him? Is there a prospect of striking a business friendship? He likes Andre's spirit and hopes he can make a lot of money with this one.

The chicken says that it will not forget the one who plucked his tail during the rainy season.

The area around the Melville Police Station bustles with activity. Police vehicles pull in and out of the parking spaces. It could be because it is high noon, and there is an ongoing change in duty shifts.

Osas steps out from his taxi, pays the driver,

and approaches the police station. He runs a mental check one more time. Sure enough, he has nothing incriminating on him. He has not come with a stash of cocaine. There is no pistol in the waistline of his jeans and his papers are up to date. He is sure Officer Kungawo would not be on duty at this time. Today is the man's day off. In any case, he has not come to see the man. Asuquo was arrested the night before. Bystanders say the police had become suspicious of him. They had cornered him, and he had fled after ramming straight into one of the police officers and knocking him down. The other police officer tore after him and caught him only after Asuquo had successfully lost his stash of cocaine. Now he is in the station for assaulting a police officer.

Osas heads to the front desk. He tells the woman behind the counter why he is visiting, and she gives him a form to fill out then instructs him to take a seat on one the padded benches in the waiting area. He sits a few meters from a man in handcuffs. Osas watches him from the corner of his eyes. The man looks uncomfortable in the cuffs. His business suit and glasses make him look out of place. There is no telling his nationality, but he sure is not from South Africa. Osas turns to the man, wanting to throw a word of greeting, maybe start a conversation. The man looks away, avoiding his eyes, as he does with everyone else.

A few others wait in the area as well. Some look like they have come to see someone, just like him. One seems like he is waiting to file a complaint. There is no one else in cuffs besides the man on Osas's right.

A man is dragged into the station, screaming threats. The police officers grabbing him do not want him to have all the attention, so they shout back, matching threat with threat. Every eye turns to them. From the insults traded back and forth, Osas gathers that the man, a local, had set fire to his ex-girlfriend's house. The woman escaped despite sustaining burns. The man has done this because he could not bear the sight of her with a new boyfriend.

She is a bitch, he yells, vowing to do much worse after his release.

Why are men in South Africa this way, Osas wonders? Incidents like this are always in the news. Perhaps it is good, after all, to travel and see things as they are, how different the world is from what one is used to.

The woman in the police uniform calls his name. "Follow me," she says.

She leads him along a corridor to a wide room. Two metal benches welded into the floor stand opposite each other, with a table in between.

"Sit here," she says. "Your friend will be with you in a moment."

Soon, a police officer leads Asuquo in. His hands are cuffed in front. The police officer guides him onto the bench then stands stiffly at the entrance. "Five minutes," he tells them.

"How far?" Osas asks Asuquo.

Asuquo gives him an assuring smile. "No shaking."

"Shebi you no dey loaded when them hold you?"

"Them no see anything."

"Confirm. I say make I come see you. Me and men for hood dey this morning. Them tell me wetin happen. Everybody go contribute money find you better lawyer. We go find you Pink lawyer, wey go comot you ASAP. So make you no worry. You get love for street."

"Una correct. God go bless una."

"No wahala. I go drop something for you in case you need anything. You know as e dey be na."

Asuquo is moved to tears. He hisses and shakes his head.

Osas pats him on the shoulder. "No worry, my man. You be good person. You no dey give wahala. We gats dey your back."

"Time's up!" the policeman announces. He comes around and helps Asuquo to his feet, then leads him away.

Osas remains seated for a while longer. It is a tough thing to be remanded behind bars in a foreign country, he reasons. If ever such a fate is to befall him, God forbid, he hopes it will not be for any serious offence. Good thing he pays Officer Kungawo as added insurance, just in case. Besides, Papi is not one to let any of his boys pine away in some police cell. He is always happy to pay a bribe for their release, but the fellow remains indebted to him, sometimes for twice the amount against which the release was secured.

At the reception desk, Osas asks to see the chief guard on duty. He banks in three hundred rands in Asuquo's name before leaving. He walks a considerable distance, hails a taxi, and calls out his destination to the driver. He has to see Chike so that they can go remit cash to Papi and get fresh supplies of cocaine.

Protea Hotel by Marriot Johannesburg Parktonian stands prominent on a street corner in Braamfontein, on De Korte Street. You can see its towering roof from a considerable distance away. Its elegance beckons and imposes all at once. On a normal day, the neighbourhood is a beehive of activities, from cars and taxis pulling up at the entrance, to guests arriving and departing as porters attend to their luggage. It gets busier when its halls are used for events and conferences.

It is the first time Osas is entering any Protea Hotel. He has taken the time to dress well in a black suit and silver tie. He wants to look the part of a respectable guest so that he does not stand out. No one is to suspect that he is carrying cocaine. That would earn him a long time in jail. Some fellows are having an indoor party in one of the executive suites. One of them is an acquaintance of Papi's and a respected customer at the club.

Papi has sent Osas to make sure the guests never run out of cocaine.

He had thought Chike would be asked to accompany him, but Papi had another very important task for Chike.

The entrance of the building looks elegant. The rug on the steps feels like a cushion beneath the soles of his shoes. The attendants tip their heads to him. For once, he thinks he gets a taste of what it feels like to be rich and important. Right past the rotating doors and into the building, the serenading opulence envelopes him. It makes him feel small. He realises that the exterior of the building is only the tip of the iceberg compared to the sights and senses inside. He cannot tell how long he stands rooted in his unhidden admiration of the place, but someone greets him, jolting him back to reality. It is a porter, a young lad. Twenty, maybe.

"Sorry, please, where is Suite 304?"

"Please come with me to the reception area, sir. You'll be attended to," the porter says, leading the way.

Osas follows him.

At the reception desk, the smartly dressed women behind the gleaming marble counter attend to three women. One of the guests stands out from the rest. His bulky frame is garbed in a traditional brightly patterned robe. He types into his phone with keen concentration. One of the receptionists waits patiently on him, a warm smile on her pretty face.

"You're welcome, sir," another receptionist says to Osas, as he draws up to the counter.

It is then that the bulky man looks up.

Osas can tell he is gazing intently at him. Their eyes lock.

"You?" the man says, pointing at him with bewilderment in his eyes. "It's you! This bloody Nigerian!"

Osas's heart skips a beat.

Hell!

It is Chief Nosakhare. There is no time to talk or make room for further drama. There is no telling what the man will do to him as soon as he recovers from the initial shock of coming face to face with him in the most unlikely place on earth.

Osas flees, out through the winding door, down the wide steps with the red rug, and onto the streets.

Everything has returned to normal. Every day looks the same, with the same issues of selling cocaine and meeting targets, making deliveries, running errands for Papi, remitting cash and getting new supplies. There has been a little difference, though.

Osas has not been in touch with April lately. They had quarrelled over the fact that he gives her little attention, and she accused him of using work as an excuse to avoid her. He has been seeing little of

Madam Ruth, too, as Papi hardly leaves town these days.

It has been one whole week since the incident at the Protea Hotel.

⁕

If you hurry to dig and cut up a yam, you must bend down and dig up its tail.

As Osas promised Asuquo, they hired a pink lawyer, a man who said he was Jewish and that the Jews in South Africa are successful and do not lose cases in courts.

Oh yes, he was right.

Asuquo was released from prison. There was mild partying.

However, the monotony of daily life is interrupted when Asuquo meets Osas at an outdoor café. They are not close pals. Instead, they are mere acquaintances and often run into each other in the line of business. Asuquo makes small deals. He has no bosses, answerable to no one. Still, he has not made it big, does not drive a posh car, and does not live in a rich neighbourhood. It is a wonder that he has not been run down by the competition. Maybe because he is a nice person and never gives anyone trouble.

Asuquo had asked to meet with a hint of urgency in his tone. For once, feeling sceptical, Osas has chosen a public venue, where they can be amongst ordinary folks.

"Some people dey find you for Jo'burg," Asuquo tells him without wasting time.

A waiter comes around, and Asuquo orders coffee for them both. The interruption by the waiter has allowed Osas enough time to absorb his initial surprise.

"Why them dey find me?" Osas asks soon as the attendant moves out of earshot.

Asuquo holds out his hands in a gesture that shows he is clueless. "Somebody don put price for your head. Them say na twenty thousand rands for anybody wey go bring your head."

"So if person collect my head, who them go carry am give?"

Asuquo laughs and cracks his knuckles.

He looks like one who has been cornered. "You be sharp guy. That's why I dey like your way."

He leans closer in his seat, dropping his voice down to a bare whisper. "Na one chief for Jo'burg. Them say him dey very important. Everybody sabi am."

Osas feels like he has been hit with a

sledgehammer. He wonders why he is surprised that Chief Nosakhare put the hit on him. The server returns to their table. She sets down the coffee and leaves with her tray.

"But wetin you do this man?"

Osas contemplates whether to go into the details of the chance, but a brief encounter that had brought him face to face with, and into the bad books of, Chief Nosakhare.

Where should he start?

From the trip to Jo'burg to babysit some absurd idea of Papi's?

Should he start from the girl, Sophie, who was always making overt advances on him until he had asked himself what he stood to lose if he gave in for a moment?

She was exceedingly pretty and looked rich, too.

A subtle wild one. She had gotten a taste of cocaine and would never let go. He had profited immensely but she had deteriorated until she had ended in a rehabilitation centre. Only then did the truth about her true identity became known to Osas—she was a new bride of the prominent Chief Nosakhare, who had paid heavily to bring her over from Swaziland and make her his wife.

Osas wanted to leave the city after he was told

that the furious chief was asking questions about him.

He does not tell Asuquo any of this. "Na bad business," he tells him instead.

Later that same night, Chike confronts Osas again with the news.

"Them dey find you for Jo'burg," he says in a matter-of-fact voice. "Very soon them fit find you enter Braamfontein."

They are sorting out currency notes after the day's sales. The business has been fair for the night.

"You gats do something because the money them put for your head plenty o. You know say niggas dey hungry for town."

""Wetin I go do?" Osas asks as he rolls a little wad of money and secures it with an elastic band.

"So you no know?"

"No. I no know."

"Find the man wey put the hit on you."

Osas looks at him with a hint of disbelief. "Wetin I go tell am when I meet am?"

"You no need tell am anything. Just light am up."

Osas falls silent. Chike may be right. He has always known at the back of his mind that a time will come when the search for him will become so intense that he will have to be on the run for the rest of his life. He had considered telling Papi about it and ask for protection even though it would come at a price he would surely not be able to pay for a very long time, if ever at all. Chike presents him with the best option. Yes, he will have to take a trip to Jo'burg and kill the man.

That is the only way to save his life. Since nobody will be paying for his head, no one will come seeking for it either.

Like they say; if a person goes and gets one whole measure of oil to eat only one yam, does he think the yam farmer who owns the land would put aside a whole mortar of palm fruit for oil?

THE ALLIANCE

Either the Nigerian has distorted sense of humour or he is just plain delusional, Chamai thinks as he stares dumbfounded at Chike. They are inside an Our Blend coffee shop, which always has sparse patrons. Chike watches the disgust growing on Chamai's face with amusement.

"What the fuck, man?"

"Exactly," Chike agrees with a smile. "I bring the men, you fuck the men. We both gon make lots of money. Isn't that what you need? Money?"

"Not that kind of money! I thought you could help me to get my taxi license," Chamai says, exasperated. "You said that you know important men."

Nodding, Chike takes a sip from his cup. "Yes, I do, and I want you to fuck them for me. You are a good-looking boy. You can play this game."

Chike says, "Why do you these guys like taking and not giving anything back?"

Chamai runs a hand through his hair. "I can't do that! I didn't come to South Africa to put up my ass for auction."

Chike chuckles and then gets up, tossing fifty rands on the table. "In case you change your mind, the number I give you."

Chamai stares at Chike, in disbelief as he walks out of the coffee shop. Then he looks at the fifty rands, lying on the table, and feels as if he is going to be sick.

"Why do Nigerians disrespect people?" he mutters to himself.

⁕

Inside a Burger King, Osas stares blankly at Andre, who sits across from him, sipping from a bottle of Valpre spring water.

"C'mon Osas," Andre says. "Let's cut the back and forth." He glances around to confirm that their privacy is being threatened. "Hook me up with the good stuff. Then you have a regular customer on your hands. I can afford it. So? Can you?"

Osas looks Andre straight in the eye and then makes his decision. "You sabi Sumo Nightclub?"

A smile creeps onto Andre's lips. "I know most of the Nigerian hangouts around here."

Osas tells Andre about the KY barbing saloon on Juta Street. "Meet me there by eight."

Andre flashes Osas a grin. "So you got a number I can call or something?"

"Not necessary," Osas says. "Just come to Sumo Nightclub. You go see me there!"

"Huh?"

"Just come. You go see me when you get to the club," Osas says, getting to his feet.

Chamai walks consciously, along the empty hallway of his flats in the flickering light of the naked bulb, up to his door. He stealthily attempts to open it, but the door across from his bursts open. The middle-aged landlady, some giant of a woman in her pink nightdress, steps onto the hallway.

"Hello," Chamai says sheepishly.

"You can keep your hellos. All I want is my rent!" she charges. "Every day you crawl back at night and crawl out first thing in the morning to avoid me. But today I catch you!"

Chamai swallows hard.

"My rent, my rent!" the woman says, shouting

in his face now. "It is three months now, and I must get it!"

"I'll get it for you next week."

"Last week you said next week."

"You'll get it this time, I swear. Next week," Chamai tries to reassure her.

She regards Chamai, unconvinced.

"I promise, Anochengeta," he says more softly.

"You sure? Because me I am tired of your next week, next week. Next week Monday, Chamai. Or you are on the street. Even if you are from Zim, too."

"I promise," he says once more.

"Okay. But I *will* kick you out, Chamai. I have children to feed."

"There won't be a need for that," he says as he opens his door and glides inside.

Not bothering to turn on the lights, Chamai sits down on the floor against the wall. He knows Anochengeta meant every word of her threat and that he will have to try to find a way to take care of the rent. The embarrassment is becoming too much, and he does not want be homeless. He takes a deep breath and then reluctantly opens an email on his phone, the last of his possessions now that his watch and wallet are gone. The email is from Damelin. There is Damelin College there in Braamfontein.

Dear Mr. Chamai Mangezi,

This is to remind you that you have just one-week's grace left to pay your deferment fees for this academic year. Failure to pay within the next seven days will result in a permanent forfeiture of your continued admission to our institution.

Chamai sighs deeply and then buries his face in his hands.

His shoulders rocks as he sobs. Things are spinning fast. It is all too much for him. It is more than he can keep up with, more than he can control. He replays all the trials of his life—how he was thrown into the whirlpool of fate, the blows that came along with it, and the resolution with which he was expected to navigate through it all.

Raised the Shona way, Chamai had spent most of his life in a remote village in the Zaka District after his mother had returned from Canada without his father. Chamai was four, then. The soil had been as hard as the stones on top of it. Electricity was a fantasy that no one expected to come true. The simplest illness could sweep away as many lives as it wanted before a doctor would eventually reach them from the city. His mother's supreme devotion had been to her maize and yam farm and, with her fat arms; she had worked until she lost her breath.

Anokos had been ill tempered with her son, Chamai because the laborious work on the farm always seemed too much for him. However, Chamai knew her impatience for him stemmed from the grudge she held against his father who had left for another woman.

Her father, Takura, had been ill for as long as Chamai could remember. The lean old man would lay in bed almost the whole day, snoring or talking to himself in his sleep and when he did come out to "catch the sun", he would settle down in his armchair, drinking *hwahwa* and smoking his pipe. People said that he was once the most respected stone carver in these parts and that his former wife (who had died before Chamai was born) had poisoned him after a fiery argument. The medicine, everyone said, was what had rendered him so ill.

Chamai loved the man. At every opportunity, when there were not chores and necessities of farm life to be dealt with, he would sit with his grandfather and discuss anything and everything. Not only did the old man regale Chamai with stories from his past, but he would also explain abstract ideas like the mechanics of the natural world and the dynamics of human relations. The old man had not been a very good farmer and had managed to avoid the arduous labour by turning a tidy profit with his stone carvings. He encouraged Chamai to pursue words instead of maize and yam. A special bond existed between the old man and boy. In this way, life on the farm became entirely bearable for Chamai, who began to excel at schoolwork from an early age.

Chamai had attended the school set up by the Methodist church. His academic performance had been outstanding; his teachers had boasted that his future was so bright that you needed sunglasses to look at it. One day, close to his final exams, Chamai's joy of being alive turned to dust. A small group of locals crowded in his grandfather's bedroom. On the mattress lay the skeletal old man. His eyes were shut, his half-naked body, limp. In the corner, his mother sobbed, and two elderly women were stroking her back. The air stank of misery.

"Ndine hurombo," a distant uncle said to him, his voice barely audible. "He fought well and hard."

Chamai said nothing. The suddenness of the loss had sent him into a state of shock. It was not until he walked away, into the maize field, that the tears began to fall. He felt as if they would never stop. It was his first experience with the death of a relative, someone he loved dearly. In the days and weeks that followed, a great depression found its way into his spirit and made him numb to the world.

After his grandfather's funeral, Chamai's mother threw herself into her farm work harder than ever before. She worked as though ploughing the field was her way of breaking free from her sorrows. It was as if nothing else mattered to her anymore.

Chamai had written his final exams at the Zaka community secondary school and his grades were far below the expectations. All of his teachers wondered how a boy as brilliant as he could have made such a hash of his exams. They knew his grandfather had passed away, but still—it was only his grandfather, not his father!

Some of his schoolmates, who had also performed poorly in their exams, returned to the markets, where they were often seen hawking foodstuffs. Chamai knew he would have to join his mother in the struggle to eke out a living. That did not appeal to him.

He longed for much more. In an act of desperation, he applied to a technical college in South Africa with a cover letter that tried to explain the circumstances of his bad grades. For weeks, Chamai remained idle, clueless about what to do with himself. His mother, as always, spent her time on the farm. Some of his close friends from the small village had gone off to Harare or Bulawayo for their admissions to prestigious universities, and here he was, wasting away, in a house riddled with ancient cobwebs, termites, and memories.

Chamai would have gone crazy from frustration, but then, a letter arrived in the mail, notifying him of his acceptance. There was no need to tell his mother, who would offer nothing but indifference. He had to protect the small chance he now had to escape. There was no future for him anywhere in the village, and this community seemed perpetually doomed to be retrogressive. He had even heard rumours that the mission school would soon be shut down. He needed to leave.

Three months after his final exams, Chamai did what he had initially considered unthinkable—he joined some of his classmates in hawking, asking them to help him get started in the trade. He was pleasantly surprised that whatever wares he had sold out, and he was soon able to pay back his classmates and purchase his own. He understood the reason behind his luck, too. Many people in the village knew him, and his scholarly genius was a near-legend in these parts. People had bought from him out of fascination, striking up conversations, wondering why a promising lad like him would settle for the life of the uneducated. Chamai merely smiled and told them what they wanted to know. It was important for the business to move fast. People did not realise that they were both patronising and aiding him that once he had earned enough, he would disappear to seek his Golden Fleece. As soon as Chamai had sufficient cash to fund his travel and schooling expenses, he disappeared.

One morning, Chamai's mother finally noticed that her son and his clothes were no longer there. She was beside herself with horror. She noticed he letter placed on the wooden stool in the kitchen. It said he had joined a crew marching band that was determined to cross the border, and that he was sorry, very sorry, but he was irrevocably bound for South Africa and a better life. She read the letter then simply went back out into the field to continue farming. Though she hated to admit it, that day would be the one that separated all the others from those to come. She wished her only son a better life than what she had been able to give him. She wished she had tried harder. Then, like everything else, she tried to forget.

So here was Chamai, in this strange country

and city, being made an offer to fuck other men, an offer that made him feel sick to his stomach. He was helpless. Turning this proposal down would be foolish. He had already tried hawking, but between the hostile locals who believed it was only for South Africans and the local gang who harassed him endlessly, it had proved impossible. The college he had enrolled in was interested only in taking money, not giving it out. No grants. No scholarships. Nowhere to look for financial assistance. Soon he would run out of money for food. Chike's telephone number was the only option. He stared at it for longer than he had ever looked at anything in his entire life.

That same night on Juta Street, a stream of foreign men enter and leave the KY barbershop. A few men hang around outside, smoking and chattering loudly about Nigerian football teams and the upcoming African Cup of Nations.

Inside, Kayode, a handsome and annoyingly boisterous fellow, has just finished cutting a customer's hair. He looks at the customer in the mirror and smiles to himself. He is starting to get the hang of this haircutting business. He dabs aftershave on the customer's chin.

"Baba mi, see as you set finish! But how e no go fine, when na de world KY handle you? You go top something for your boy, jare!"

Smiling, the customer hands him the bill, with a small tip.

"Na so! E sure for you, baba, eshe gan."

Just as the customer exits the shop, Chike enters. He and Kayode engage in a peculiar handshake that ends with the snapping of their fingers.

"The world KY!" Chike hails. "How e dey happen?"

"Normal level, baba. I still never get Barclays credit card. I don lose better client this week, e pain me gan.

"Na wetin make you go dey ask that Bucket man for account?" Chike asks.

"Baba me, any way na way oh! Meanwhile, them Moses still de wait. You don get buyer?"

"Buyer dey ground."

Kayode says, "And me personally get Gucci bags plenty. Na to find fence troway them for black market sharperly."

Andre enters through the front door, a warm smile on his lips. Both Chike and Kayode turn to him with stone faces. The men standing outside watch him through the window, equally serious.

"Wanna cut?" Kayode asks, whipping up the electric razor.

"Actually, I'm here to meet someone," Andre replies, nervously. "A guy called—"

"I'm here," Osas announces, emerging from an inner room, and slapping Chike on the back.

Chike is startled. "Osas! Where you waka enter since?"

"Hustling." Osas turns to Andre. "Let's go."

The moment Osas and Andre leave the shop, Kayode releases a deep breath. "Hustle ke?"

Chike and Osas smile at one another. At that moment, Chike's phone rings. He fishes in his pockets for it and swipes the screen. "Yeah, who be this?" A smile crosses his face. "I happy now say you see this from my angle, Chamai. Call me tomorrow by four. I tell you where we meet."

Outside as they are strolling along the busy street, Osas hands the cocaine packet cocaine to Andre. He had received the same packet earlier that day from Don Papi. He nods when Andre slips him a thick wad of cash, which he glances at and flips through, before safely putting it away in his pocket.

"It's all there," Andre reassures him. "Wouldn't wanna fuck with you guys. This stuff had better be good, though. My clients are top shelf."

Osas merely smiles at Andre.

They bump their fists together and head off in different directions. Osas knows that an important alliance has just been forged. Things are looking up.

They say a leopard cannot to get rid of its spots. The same is true for Osas. His childhood always comes back to haunt him. He sees it play before his eyes, in his waking thoughts, sober moments and whenever he has time to ponder in solitude. There are times he fears the events of his childhood will somehow plague his life again.

School was not the same for Osas as the other children. This much, he was sure. It was evident, from their discussions, that they had lives, which he could only live in his most wishful fantasies. While they had parents who spoiled them with attention, he had a grandmother who was disgruntled from the very moment he came to know her.

A kid once said his father would whip him if he did not improve his second-place ranking in the class. The kid's dad had whipped him for scoring 25% on the last test. Osas had wondered what it would be to live like that kid.

"Na so my Papa dey do," another kid said. "One

day, my mama tell am 'make you no kill my son o! You be man, you no sabi wetin e be to carry pikin for belle for nine months. You don enter labour room before?' Na so my papa say, 'na so una dey spoil children. After now, una go dey cry say pikin don spoil finish.'"

Osas's grandmother only allowed him to go to school because the community school was very cheap. In addition, she would not be able to stand the neighbourhood gossip if she stopped him from going. She never cared how he did his academic performance was the least of her concerns.

During lunch breaks, he often had nothing to eat. While everyone got out his or her own lunchboxes, he would take a stroll around the classroom block instead. It was better than to be tormented by the aroma of foods that was soon to fill the classrooms. As he waited in the corridor by the window of a class, he overheard some kid tell another. "The rice and stew wey my mama cook yesterday, eh. Na so I chop sotay my belle want burst."

Once, an outstandingly neat boy had said, "My mum washes my uniform every Saturday. She says I do not know how to do it well. The way she'll soak the white shirts in water and bleach on Friday night ... On Saturday, she'll wash, put in starch and blue, then when they dry, she will iron ... Every time, she tells me 'cleanliness is next to godliness.'"

The words had seared into Osas's soul. Why did he not have parents like other boys? What sins had he committed against the Almighty to deny him what everyone else had? He was bitter at fate, bitter at his absent parents and especially at the implacable presence in his life: his grandmother.

On the day when one of his classmates taunted him, "You no get Papa or Mama," Osas had attacked the boy in homicidal rage. That day he realised how easily one could commit murder. He could have pummelled and ripped the life out of that boy without a flicker of remorse. The teachers had to pry him from the poor boy.

Later, left alone, Osas had sobbed long and hysterically.

SINS OF LIFE

Don Papi is sailing on the highest levels of ecstasy. His thighs quiver uncontrollably as he groans in pure and final delight. This has been a unique and glorious experience. Her tongue has been slithering in practised dexterity around his cock. It had been like a velvet snake exploring new territories. In addition, she stops just at the right moment, before it becomes too sensitive, and looks him in the eye. Such eyes! They have a dreamy and satisfying expression to them. His mind has been blown away at this woman's abilities.

"*Nne*, you wan make me run mad?" he breathes out, panting.

Ruth smiles satisfactorily, takes two Kleenex from the table. "Na hand touch you! Nineteen years for the business no be puff puff."

They are at the desk, half-clad. Don Papi lights up a cigarette and takes a couple of drags, staring off into nowhere as he lets out a steady stream of smoke. "That one dey. How your new girls?"

"Them dey do well," she says, putting her bra back on. "But I dey watch that Angela."

"Wetin she do?" he asks, not because he cares. The least you could give the woman is a little bit of conversation afterwards.

"I hear say she get university degree. You know say those ones dey believe say one day them go find Prince Charming." There is contempt in her voice.

Papi snorts. Someone buzzes from the outer security gate. He quickly pulls up his trousers and stares at the monitor. It is the new boy, Osas.

Don Papi watches the screen, settling himself comfortably on the chair. Ruth buttons up her blouse. Someone knocks on the door.

"Oya enter," Papi says and pushes the buzzer.

Osas marches in, past Ruth without a glance in her direction, and dumps a gold bracelet and a thick wad of cash on the desk. He has the air of a man who is proud of his achievement.

Papi regards the loot with a measure of incredulity. Then he glances at Ruth who has a smile on her face, and then at Osas. Osas stiffens at Don Papi's stare. Averting his gaze, he looks to his right and Ruth. Recognition flashes through his countenance. She was the woman at the mall who had vanished with his wristwatch!

"You no fit greet?" Papi snarls.

"Good evening, boss," Osas, says to Papi, unthinkingly, and then turns to Ruth. "Where my watch?"

Papi casts puzzled glances at the two of them.

"Na watch suppose dey there, boss," Osas explains. "She help me move am comot for Edgars, but I no see her as I comot outside."

Wordlessly, Ruth picks up her white purse from the table and pulls out a wristwatch. Osas had stowed the same one away in her purse. Nonchalantly, she drops the object next to the money and the bracelet.

"Don Papi," she says, "Them almost catch am dey shoplift. Lucky for him, I dey around there. Na, the new boy be this?"

Papi nods. "Yeah, na the guy. But Osas, no dey do like rookie at all." He picks up the watch and inspects it. "All the *white* don go?"

"Yes boss."

"Where Chike dey?"

In perfect synchronicity, Papi's security buzzer

sounds. Chike is looking up at the camera. Papi lets him in.

Chike walks into the room and casts Osas a condescending look before attending to the big man. "Good afternoon, boss." He turns to Ruth, charismatically. "Madam Ruth, I hail."

She smiles at him.

"This village boy been dey hustle," Papi says.

"Na wetin e talk when I see am one eye now now for KY shop. Him wey no know anywhere. Na mouth e get. No respect and little sense," Chike says, disdainfully.

"See him work," Papi gestures to the loot. "Even you no been sharp like this, you need respect the boy."

Chike frowns. He may as well have just been spat on.

"Carry am go back your side. But give am drink for bar downstairs. Him deserves am," Papi orders.

Chike grinds his teeth, glares at Osas, and then storms out of the office. Osas slowly follows him, smiling.

"Chike no like the boy," Ruth says when they are alone.

"I like whoever makes me rich," Papi replies. He has long mastered the art of playing his subordinates against one another, to keep them on their toes, and get the best out of them.

Ruth smiles. She has heard that before. It was not the tone that she liked, but rather the profound truth it held. She, too, liked the girls who brought her the most money. For Ruth, it was not about affection or respect, the kind of feeling you developed towards comrades or kin. It was the purposeful using of people to your own ends—that is what mattered. All her girls were but so many bits of toilet paper; after you have used it to wipe yourself; you flush it away without second thoughts.

She knew her girls. They were at her mercy, and she showed them small affections so that they would do anything to stay in her favour. There was Ese, one of her favourites, whose real name was Okeneghese. She was Ishan and having lost her mother before she turned seven, had been condemned to watch her father fall into a faithful relationship with liquor. There had been barely anything to eat at home, and she had been compelled to start hawking boiled corn and pears. Then, as is the case with so many of the girls, she had met some married man who went by the name of Chris, who lured her with money until eventually, she went along with him to a modest guesthouse where he deflowered her. The affair lasted for a while, with him promising her the world and showering her with false affections. When they both learned she was heavy with child, he simply took off, leaving no traces of his whereabouts.

It was shortly after giving birth that Ese met Efosa, an old friend, who told her about the promises that awaited her across the borders of their country. It was an irresistible temptation, the thought of going to South Africa to work. She left her baby with her sister and for greener pastures, to the life she had always dreamed of. By the time she realised she was bound to become a sex worker, there was no way for her to rebel against her predicament. Death was the only way out now.

Ruth also knew a lot about April who, on her first attempt to go to Italy, had been attacked, by armed robbers who knew that these poor hopeful people often took their life savings with them. She had been gang-raped, as the youngest and most beautiful girl in the group. Something in her spirit had broken that day. Even though she had given up and wanted only to die, the rest of the survivors had managed to return her to her family. A few months later, she had seduced a Local Government Chairman into making her his mistress. The man was just part of April's plan, a stepping-stone towards a larger goal.

The Chairman had rented an apartment for her, bought her expensive clothing, and taken her along to private parties, where she willingly engaged in explicit sexual acts. The moment he gave her a pair of diamond earrings she had pleaded for, she was on a flight to South Africa, hunting for a new life. She had met Ruth in her second week of hunting for work. When the older woman had asked if April wanted to join the escort agency, there was no hesitation on April's part.

A week had not even passed under Ruth's care when April was introduced to Richard Montana. The attractive American businessman in his late forties was visiting the brothel for the first time and wanted a girl who could give him special treatment, for which he was more than willing to pay. April was Ruth's obvious selection. She was then sent to a remote lodge in the Karoo.

The man was very attractive, but April quickly learned there was nothing attractive about his taste in sex. He had shut the front door to the lodge and April had approached him, eager to please, but the man had clutched her by the throat. "You gonna be my slave bitch tonight, you fucking slut! Now get on your knees!"

When April had stared at him in horror, he landed an unexpected and hard slap, across her face. The viciousness of it made her eyes go starry and sent her crashing to the ground.

"What are you looking at me for, whore?" Montana had snarled when April turned to face him through her daze. "I said get on your fucking knees!"

The moment April got hold of herself; she sprung to her feet in fury, blinded by rage, maddened by humiliation and shame. "Shuoo! Na fuck you want abi na fight you come!" she had screamed hysterically, lunging towards him.

He slapped her again, harder, sending her sprawling to the floor once more. "I'm gonna choke you, bitch. I'm gonna spank you, whip you, and then I'm gonna fuck you like you've never been fucked in your life!" he towered over her, shouting.

The fight had gone out of April, but she still managed to spit at him. "No be me you go handle like thief. No be me you go handle like thief. No be my body."

Montana had smiled, an evil smile, and begun to take off his belt. "I like a stubborn bitch. Now let's start breaking you in." He drew his hand, the belt making a cracking sound through the air.

Afterwards, Ruth and the other girls nursed April back to health. Upon hearing what had happened, Ruth got so mad that she broke one of her favourite vases. April was her favourite object in the brothel, though, and the girl's sweet juicy cunt had just made her a small fortune. She had apologised to April for what had happened and showered her with affection, even going so far as to promise to find the American and get revenge. Of course, nothing came of it, but April always appreciated the gesture from Ruth.

When you walk into April's room, you will see all kinds of pictures glued to the walls—of Oprah Winfrey, Beyoncé, and Tiwa Savage. She also has Angelique Kidjo's pictures. Recently, she added Miriam Makeba and Yemi Alade. She never misses *The Oprah Show*. She once told Madam Ruth that she thought Oprah was the most powerful woman on earth. Ruth had not liked that.

"Let her come and help your life then, useless girl," Ruth snapped.

That year, Oprah was supposed to be coming to Johannesburg for the Global Citizen Festival, along with Jay Z and Beyoncé. Johannesburg was eager to welcome them. In Braamfontein, April dreamt she could meet Oprah and tell her how much she loved her. All her life, even while she was in Nigeria, she had dreamed of becoming like Oprah.

Then one day, she started an argument with the other girls. "Only if every woman is as strong as Oprah," she said. "Equality will be real. She dey siddon where men dey sit."

That evening, April had argued that women should stop changing their surnames after they marry, that Igbo women in Nigeria should never accept dowries, and the women in South Africa should not go along with lobola.

"It makes women look like slaves or goats being bought," she said. However, of course, the women did not agree with her. "Women never agree!" April shouted in frustration.

She was shocked at herself for shouting. Things had changed, she said to herself. She was in a new country, and she must look out for herself. She tried her best to calm down. In her head, she told herself that there would never be equality because of the way women behave. In bed, she lay on her back. She cried, fat tears rolling down her cheeks.

April remembered how Mr Zikomo died in the xenophobic attack last year in Honeydew, where he lived, among other Malawians in a dingy house. Mr Zikomo ran his business of forging travel documents for people from Nigeria, Ghana, Kenya and Ethiopia. He could make any passport. As soon as these people overstayed their visas, a few thousand rands would get them new visas glued to their passports. The visas looked original, but they never were. Ruth would send April to go with the new girls to get new documents, should in case the South African Police come nosing around.

Mr Zikomo would tell April whenever foreigners were attacked and robbed by South Africans. "South Africans are scared of you Nigerians," he would say. "That is why they do not attack areas occupied by you."

Mr Zikomo's body was found in the tiny room where he forged travel documents for his fellow foreigners.

"When they come to kill," Mr Zikomo had once told April, "they first kill we Malawians and then the Zimbabweans. They fear you Nigerians because you guys defend yourselves with serious weapons."

There was one girl above all the others who exerted immense psychological power over Ruth:

Angela from Onitsha. She had gotten herself murdered. Her mistake had been the ruinous act of mixing business with pleasure. Ruth knew very well how this kind of silly romance could potentially end. She had lost several girls this way. Previously, she had tried to instil fear into the girls, to coerce them into facing the facts of their dismal lives. However, it had not worked with Angela.

Angela had fallen in love with a John, some white chap from Cape Town. The thrill of love had made her forget herself. She had secretly rented an apartment in the city and then the next thing; everyone had heard that someone had put a bullet through her forehead. Her death made the other girls cling more tightly to Ruth, which reassured her of her influence and control over her sex empire.

Ruth knew the peaks that anguish could scale. She hated to think about where she had come from, the things she had done. However, she invariably did, and her past would come sweeping over her like a wave and with it came a tumbling, drowning pain. To avoid this feeling, she remained slightly inebriated for most of the day, every day.

Her life back in Benin City had been a suffocating nightmare. Shortly before she had given birth to sweet Omorogie at the age of sixteen, her father, the street-painter bastard, had taken off. The ridicule she had faced had been devastating. Her mother had introduced her to a person called Babel James. Through the curtains of the sitting room one day, she had watched this man give her mother a small wad of cash that could not have amounted to very much. Babel James then took her to some shrine along Agbor road and at midnight, she and one other girl were forced to stand naked, in the crippling cold. A priestess, ringed eyed in a white robe, had come and given them a calabash with some liquid in it to drink. Ruth drank it, with the priestess waving a palm frond over her. It had tasted like sour wine. Then, half a dozen young men with stern expressions had emerged from the shadows. The violation that had happened to her had less to do with her body that night than her soul.

Suffering was part of the journey to glory. Ruth understood that now. She did not look upon the suffering of her girls as a negative thing, but rather as her way of helping them to find glory as she had done for herself.

When Ruth arrived in South Africa, through arrangements made by Babel James, she had been introduced to Papi. Through Papi, she knew she was going to attain great power. She was going to be successful, for the sake of her baby, who she had left with his grandmother and who she would one day go back to find. Now her successes in the world of sex were the stuff of legend among the Nigerian diaspora. For this to pass, Ruth had needed to bury Omorogie in her heart.

Chike is drumming his fingers on the table in Our Blend coffee shop when Chamai, wearing a thick oversized blue sweater, approaches him, pulls out a seat, and sits down.

"I think say you don chicken out," he says, smiling.

"My landlady was just outside my door," Chamai explains.

Chike's brows tilt upwards in confusion. "So?"

"I owe three months' rent, man."

"Right," Chike says, comprehending the situation. He regards Chamai critically. "You no find something sexy to wear?"

"I wore what I got, okay," Chamai answers, defensively.

"Okay, okay," Chike holds up both his hands, grinning.

"Please, Chike. Is there no other work for me?" Chamai begs.

"No other work," Chike shakes his head. "What I look like to you? Labour broker! You be Zimbo. What other work you gon do?"

"Fine. Where am I meeting him?"

Chike would forever remember Chamai's panic-stricken face as they walked down the illuminated corridor of the hotel and knocked on the door to the room. When a happy little voice from inside told them to come in, Chike merely opened the door, pushed Chamai inside, then walked away. His part of the job was done.

A night to that morning, Chike had stayed awake streaming porn videos on the internet. It was eating up his internet data, but he had ceased to mind after finishing three video clips of gay porn. He touches himself as he watched on, holding back the rushing orgasm and continuing the cycle all over again.

His taste for the male gender had been mostly closeted, but it was very much present. There was a time when such possibilities were never existent. Perhaps he could call it the age of innocence, or was it ignorance? Are they not the same thing? Of course, they should be. After all, Adam and Eve were innocent until they ate of the fruit of knowledge. They shed away ignorance and innocence was gone. It was in the Seminary in Enugu that he tasted of the fruit of knowledge and the innocence left him. Whenever he thought of this, it made him laugh. Life was truly an irony.

His parents were very religious folks, members of the Deeper Life Bible Church. Everything material or too expressive was considered sinful. Dancing in the church was too expressive too, and so considered sinful. Members were forbidden to own television sets in their houses, as it was the devil's medium for propagating perversion. Oh, and they read so much of the bible, those parts that talked of God's coming destruction of this sinful world and all the sinful people in it and taking the righteous and unsullied ones with Him to heaven. He had considered heaven to be a boring place inhabited by only people like their church members. There would not be anything to do in heaven other than to sing and clap for all eternity. What drudgery. But then if he were to choose between being destroyed by fire and boring heaven, he would rather be with the rest in heaven and escape the horrible damnation that awaited everyone on earth. With these thoughts, he had grown up until when his parents had taken him to begin his schooling in the seminary in Enugu, shortly after his twelfth birthday.

Boarding school had not been easy. He was made to wake up as early as five in the morning and take a cold bath in the open-air enclosure that served as a bathroom, with other junior students. Everything about life became regimented. Gone were the comfort of home and family. They seemed to have been torn from him without notice, and his parents, in their bid to bring him up 'in the fear of God' had thrust him into a community of other unfortunate kids whose parents thought the same thing of them. There were those elements in the student community who were there because their parents had no idea about what to do with them and so had shifted the responsibility of damage control to the school authorities. These ones were the bullies and the cause of everything that threatened to go wrong and for which the school authorities were forever on the watch.

Chike never liked the seminary. He cried most of the time and contemplated running away on more than one occasion. Things began to change when he met Odogwu. They called him Senior Odogwu. He was a senior student and the refectory prefect. A very quiet and reserved fellow, he was. It was never heard that he fell out with anyone, not even his classmates or the teachers. He never whipped or punished any students. Other junior students envied Chike because Senior Odogwu seemed to favour him. One day Senior Odogwu told him that he liked him and wanted him to be his school son. Chike agreed, and life became so much bearable for him. He was exempted from so many things. He did not wake up so early nor bathed as early as other junior boys did, and he even bathed with warm water heated in the school kitchen. It was the choicest food he ate in the refectory. Soon, Senior Odogwu asked him to share his bed with him. That way, he would be more protected, Senior Odogwu had told him. One of such nights, Senior Odogwu began to stroke Chike's penis. His hand felt oily against his limp penis, and Chike could perceive the unmistaken smell of Vaseline.

It was not the only time. Every night, they looked forward to deriving pleasure from each other in the cover of darkness and to the sound of the snores of every other inhabitant of the dormitory. They became inseparable as the days went by. The days fled in this way, just as every good thing in the world seems to fly towards an abrupt end. The abrupt end for their love came with Senior Odogwu's graduation. It was heartbreak for them both. Things never remained the same for Chike. He guessed it was same too for

Senior Odogwu, wherever he may have been upon graduation. The last time he heard from him, he was in a university in Prague, Czech Republic.

Chike went through school and much of his life like a demented fellow. He longed for a replacement for Senior Odogwu. The closest to a replacement came in the form of Samson, a smallish and junior Customs officer he had met at a bar. One would wonder how the fellow passed the recruitment process, but it had happened because he warmed the bed of an alhaji who was a Customs boss, and as compensation, the man had recruited him into his service before his transfer came through to Port-Harcourt. Just when things were beginning to look settled for both of them, Samson broke the news to Chike that he was getting married and would not want any stress on his new life. Many things had gone through Chike's mind but that night; he drank himself to stupor and wept into his pillow.

Life had gone on.

Time dragged past, and then he came to South Africa.

When he met Osas, something had come alive in him, but the guy seemed out of reach. It would require time and decisive effort to turn him around and see if things would work out. He had housed

Osas and treated him fine initially, but even at that, the guy was not easy to approach.

There seemed to be no backdoor through which he could squeeze himself into Osas and make him see the things he felt for him. Things took a turn for the worse when Osas began to bring in prostitutes. He felt like committing murder. It tore at his heart and threatened to drive him crazy. How could it be that happiness and stability would always evade him? What is wrong with the world and the people in it? Hatred and resentment for all men had gnawed in his heart. He had driven Osas out and then he had met the weakling, Chamai. He would take out his frustrations on the fellow. He knew if he approached him, like all others, Chamai would disappoint him too.

So why not let the fellow suffer?

He had to. He would do it, and there would be no mercy.

He thought of calling Chamai. It was still too early. He would give him thirty minutes and then he would call him.

They had unfinished business, and it would be for his pleasure.

Papi was on the phone, screaming when Chike walked in and sat in the chair across him. He was still talking loudly. Like they say in South Africa: Nigerians are *loud*. Chike once joked to a South African acquaintance, "Zulu and Xhosa men scream their lungs out, and that is why they are not good in bed." Chike would later think this repeatedly and never say it publicly. He knew that South Africans could say anything they want about foreigners, but foreigners are not allowed to say whatever they wish about them in their own country. "You can't abuse your host," he warned other Nigerians. It was not right.

Papi turned to him. "The case is closed."

Chike did not understand what he was talking about.

"The case of the idiot that ran away with my cut from the deal you are involved in," Papi said. "I asked them to strangle him and throw him into the waters in Cape Town."

"Cape Town?" Chike was shocked. "How did he end up in Cape Town?"

"He bought a Range Rover and a Porsche," Papi said. "He moved to Cape Town. I sent some of my smart men to go, pretending as if they wanted to make peace. They did what I asked for, and they took his laptop and phone."

Chike sat there, transfixed.

"So," Papi ordered, "make their balance available. I will give you their account details, so you can transfer their money to them."

Chike was perplexed. What was the point? How could someone owe you and you kill them, then end up paying the killers almost the same amount the person owed you? It did not make any sense. There was no logic to it.

As if Papi knew what Chike was thinking, he said, "We must pay for our sins."

"Papi, you could have given him some time to pay back," Chike said.

"No," Papi said. "I need someone to bring that Ghanaian piece of shit, Kwame, to me tonight!"

Chike did not say anything.

"You know these Ghanaians," Papi said. "They always want the world to believe that Nigerians are the only ones who are dangerous. However, look at the piece of shit. He took my girls to São Paulo and now he can't account for everything!"

"I thought the Ethiopians handled that?"

"No," Papi continued. "The Ghanaian piece

of shit convinced me that his birds will deliver the product to the cartel in São Paulo. I haven't seen my money!"

Chike was unsettled now, and mildly irritated. He hissed. "I think you should take it easy. He will come around. He only just returned from Thailand two days ago."

Papi hit his fist on the table. "I don't want those stupid Ghanaians to think they're smarter than Nigerians!"

That was when Chike buried his head in shame. He did not know what to say. He just bent his head. This is what it is about? He thought to himself.

5

AT DEATH'S DOOR

Jamz is among the most popular nightclubs in Braamfontein. Aside from its immense size and the giant colourful billboard over its entrance, it is one of those places with an ever-changing interior. Different themes were introduced periodically and, with that, new lounges, new dance floors and new bars. Pole dancers were changed every week, and different disc jockeys from all over the country came to perform. Top entertainers, from actors to rappers to models, had their pictures taken, and the lords of the crime world gathered at exclusive sections of the club, to relax and enjoy their hard-earned money. Prostitutes were in no short supply; you could find them in practically every corner, waiting for takers and watching for potential admirers.

Dancing in the thick mix of bodies and moving

to the pulsating music of the DJs are Chike and Osas. Chike is in an inexplicably joyous mood. Osas, on the other hand, has his attention distracted by two rare pinks in the club, a man with a balding head and a blond woman, standing in a corner, a glass of white wine in each of their hands. The man's eyes lock with his. He nods at Osas.

Out of nowhere, Kayode, the newly designated hairdresser of the KY barbershop, leaps onto Chike, laughing at his surprise. They go through the routine of their complicated handshake and laugh together.

"Aiye man," Kayode hails.

"Samankpe you," Chike returns. Kayode turns to Osas, who is still watching the lanky white guy and blonde woman immersed in conversation. Osas points at the white man in a not-too-obvious manner. "You sabi that guy?"

Kayode and Chike follow Osas' finger with their eyes. "Na Steve be that. Him dey run one massage parlour close to the city centre."

Chike gestures to them to look at the table to the side of the pink. He had noted a table full of other African men in a corner. Beautiful women in transparent dresses sat around the gang.

"Buccaneers. These men gather come today," says Chike.

"You dey mind those ones? Make them dey there dey squeeze face. Aiye men dey flex!" snorts Kayode.

"That one dey. But hope say you carry bull oh. Just in case," says Chike.

"Touch my waist nah," Kayode suggests, edging closer to Chike, to drive home the point that he was armed. "I no dey go farm without cutlass. Make we go sidon joor."

The duo make their way out of the dance floor to their table. Osas, with his attention still on the pinks, gestures to the man to follow him and walks towards a bathroom. He goes inside and into a cubicle, where he pretends to urinate while taking in the footfalls of those coming in and heading out. A momentary silence follows, and then he decides the time is right. He steps out to see Steve, the escort agency owner, waiting for him at one of the basins.

"How much?" Steve asks, looking at Osas in the reflection on the mirror.

"Three hundred," Osas says.

"Give me two," Steve says, taking out money and counting it quickly.

With lightning speed, Osas exchanges the cocaine for cash and heads out towards the bar for a drink.

At the bar is April, the dark-skinned chubby girl

with a pretty face, who, Chike once told him, was one of the wildest call girls in these parts. She is nursing a drink and smiles slightly when she sees Osas.

"Lime and vodka," Osas shouts above the din to the bartender.

While the bartender gets his drink, Osas notes that April is keenly looking him over. He pretends not to notice. The bartender places the drink in front of Osas, and April sidles closer.

"Why you dey always drink vodka?" she demands over the music.

She wanted to chat, Osas thinks. "No be your business."

April scoffs. "You be Ishan guy, abi?"

Osas smiles at the accuracy of her guesswork. "You no fit stay on your own?"

She blinks. "Person no fit follow you talk?"

"Why?"

"Maybe I like you," she says.

Osas is taken aback at her ease in speaking her mind. "No be wetin I comot from Benin come do for here be that."

"Yes! I know say you be Ishan guy. My name na April. Your own, nkor?"

Osas detests the sudden familiarity with which she is speaking to him.

128

"Is that your real name?" he asks, as she turns around to face the crowds on the dance floor. He notices a faint scar running down her cheek, despite the obvious make-up trying to hide it.

"Answer me first," she insists.

He breathes out. Persistent girls were not his type. The memory of sitting in the sunlight in his room with Oghogho, helping her with her painting, suddenly floods his mind. She would have had her baby by now, he thinks. "Osas. You fit call me Oscar sha."

"Osascar!" She giggles.

Osas frowns at her humour. "You no dey work?"

"I don close. I just want high small."

Osas turns away from her to look in the direction of Kayode and Chike's table. A big, bodybuilder, whom everyone calls Maskotoe, gets up and approaches the bar. At the same time, the white woman with dyed blonde hair who had been with Steve staggers drunk into his path and is about to fall when Maskotoe reaches out and catches her.

"That's my kind of man," April says sardonically. "One who catches you as you fall."

Osas says nothing to her, thinking to himself that she has watched too many Bollywood movies.

Maskotoe has wrapped his arm around the

woman and is asking her something. A tall and skinny member of the Buccaneer gang marches over, fury etched onto his face.

"You dey mad! I don pay for this bitch!" he growls at Maskotoe.

Before Maskotoe has a chance to answer, the Buccaneer lands a vicious slap to his temple.

"Kasala wan burst," April says involuntarily, apprehension flooding through her.

Recovering from the slap, Maskotoe immediately grabs a bottle off a table, smashes it on a counter, and then plunges the jagged edge at his enemy. However, the Buccaneer is quick enough to dodge and lands a punch on the side of Maskotoe's head. In a flash, Chike, Kayode and all the others join the fight and the club explodes into chaos. Instinctively, Osas grabs April's wrist and guides her out.

Later that same night, Chamai can barely steady his hand as he inserts the key into his apartment lock. His whole body is shuddering from the tears rolling down his cheeks. He is grateful that the hallway is deserted and that his landlady is asleep. He knows that a confrontation with her, at this moment, would be too much for him. The door opens, and he steps softly inside, closing and locking it as quietly as possible behind.

Forgetting that there is no electricity, he flips the light switch. He has not been able to afford electricity for two months now. He stands still in the darkness, waiting for his eyes to adjust. As soon as he can see his makeshift bed on the floor of his empty one-room apartment, he hastily undresses; throws his underwear into a bin, then goes to the bathroom. Turning on the shower, he accepts the cold water as just another addition to his pain and suffering. He sits down on the floor of the shower and lets the water wash over him. He scrubs himself and does not stop until the tears blur his vision, and his skinny arms begin to tire out. The tears mix with the water. Chamai thinks of ways to die.

Part 2

COMMUNION

I love to see a young girl go out and
grab the world by the lapels. Life is a bitch.
You've got to go out and kick ass.
— Maya Angelou

6

BLOOD AND THE LAW

Osas reclines, half-naked on the bed, his hands behind his head as he watches April slip into her green dress from the night before. He has had many women now, since the time of Oghogho, but none of them has had April's eagerness to want to please him, and her intense interest in his sensual exploration.

"Shebi you go call me?" she turns to him and asks.

This was one of the things that Osas disliked about the women that he slept with, that they would try to turn every fuck into an invitation for something more. *Shebi you go call me?* What was that supposed to mean, Osas sighs.

"I go dey busy," he replies, tactfully. He does

not want to hurt her feelings. Not right after her wholehearted attempt to pleasure him.

"So we no go talk be that?" The demand in her tone is unsettling.

"Call me later, okay. If I dey less busy I go answer."

"You no dey romantic at all." She stares at him with a hurt expression. "No need to tell you make you come walk me." She heads for the door.

"April," he calls, and when she stops without turning around, he continues, "I like you because you sharp. And you fine."

She turns to him and smiles. "I go call you later, coconut head."

Once April is gone, Osas reaches for his phone and scrolls through his messages, wondering if there is any news about the night before. He would like some distraction now and hoped that there is perhaps some errand or other from Chike and Papi. All of a sudden, the door swings open and Chike strides in.

"Baba—"

"I hope say no be my house dat bitch sleep?" Chike asks; his tone full of steel.

"Which girl?" Chike asks, noticing a painful-looking split lip that he knows not to mention.

"April, the girl wey I pass for corridor now."

Osas puts down his phone. "Wetin be the wahala? She no thief anyting."

Chike's eyes narrow. Osas can tell that he is barely managing to keep his temper in check.

"Make I just sound am give you," Chike points at Osas. "Let this be the first and last time you carry that girl come my house. Or any woman for that matter. You see this place, na me get am. You just dey squat. If you wan fuck, go pay hotel. Shebi you be hustler."

The hostility is unmistakable. "Wetin the girl really do you?" Osas asks, despite Chike's anger, thinking it a residue of the hangover and fighting from the night before.

"Open the window, tidy this place," Chike retorts, glaring at him with irritation. He walks out of Osas' room, heads to the fridge to fetch a can of Heineken and then settles himself on the edge of the kitchen counter. He takes out his phone and dials a number. "Chamai!" he shouts, as soon as the call is answered. "How e been go?" He pauses to listen. "No be so!" he shouts again. "As you finish work you suppose call me. Anyway, meet me for KY barbing saloon by four. No, five. Yes, by five. See you there." He ends the call abruptly, snaps the can open, and then winces in pain as he tries to take a sip, forgetting his lip.

Going back again to Osas' room he sees him still

in bed, messing around on his phone. "I say open the window, na toto toto dey smell for here!"

Osas has a series of his own business to attend to, as well as Chike's and Papi's. From lifting at a targeted candy shop with an oblivious teenager behind the till; to a busy restaurant with seats placed close to one another; down to regular backstreet deals and then to a new basketball court, where he needs to watch out for potential young recruits. He has just sealed off cocaine transaction with a young white Afrikaans man, in a car down the road. He cuts through an alley to get quickly back to the main road and is counting his money when he hears movements behind him. He swirls round.

Coming towards him are three members of a gang.

Three members of a gang he had been warned to avoid at all costs stalk towards him. The ruthless Francophone gang. They are responsible for the most violent crimes in the city. They murdered anybody who crossed their path, raped the girls that slighted them, and were open to carry out hits for anyone who could pay. The presence of the dark and handsome Kunta and the fierce-looking Omoro from Togo, and the funny faced Cameroonian Mboma, make his heart race. Osas is paralysed with fear.

Big Omoro immediately grabs Osas by the neck and slams him against the alley wall.

"What doin' my turf, little weasel?" Kunta asks in his thick French accent.

Osas helpless, with Omoro pinning him painfully by the neck, lets Mboma go quickly go through his pockets. Mboma grins when he finds Osas' takings for the day – a wad of cash and a couple of grams of cocaine. Mboma hands them over to Kunta, who smiles too.

"You a new Nigewian on block, eh," Kunta laughs, flicking through the money to estimate the amount.

"Yes, the pwick is," Omoro growls into Osas' face. "I've seen him with that Chike charicter."

Defiant in the face of humiliation, knowing what is about to happen to him; Osas swings a hard kick into Omoro's crotch. The big Togolese gangster holds onto his crotch and topples like a stone, with a deep groan. Osas runs.

Mboma charges immediately after him. Kunta shoves the cocaine and money into Omoro's hand and joins the chase.

Osas tries to put as much distance between

himself and his assailants as he turns one corner after another. Leaping over a ditch, and then plunging across an empty street, he turns to look back shortly and sees they are still after him in full pursuit. All of a sudden, he smacks full speed into a man coming out of a building. Both he and the man hit the ground hard, but Osas immediately springs back to his feet and carries on running. He has lost both his advantage and momentum in the collision. He can hear the pounding of his assailants' shoes against the pavement behind him. They will cut him to pieces if they get their hands on him. He glances back again and glimpses Mboma close behind. Impulsively, he ducks down another backstreet that opens to his left. Osas covers a short distance before his heart sinks as he sees before him a tall barbed-wire fence. He jumps onto the fence but knows it is useless.

Dropping back to the ground, he turns to face his attackers. In that instance a plank comes swinging and smashes against his head, knocking him to the ground. Osas has not shaken off the burst of stars that have exploded into his vision when a rain of blows come down upon him. A vision of Oghogho running away from him through the crowd at the junction back home flashes through his mind. Then from nowhere, a siren tears through the air.

Mboma and Kunta stop and turn, raising their arms when they see the two police officers jump from their vehicle, guns levelled at them and poised to shoot.

"Move away!" Officer Mufamadi, the burly dark one barks out. "Your hands on your head! Now!"

Osas is still trying to orient himself when Officer Mbalula puts handcuffs on him.

Having declined a trip to the hospital, Osas is seated in the sparsely furnished interview room of the police station, a sullen expression on his face. "I need my money. Those guys collect my money."

On the other end of the desk sits a curious Detective Booysen of the Special Operations Directorate. "There's no way your money can be recovered without you pressing charges."

Osas shakes his head for the tenth time. "No, no charges."

Detective Booysen smiles. "Tell me why exactly, Omorogie?"

"Oscar! You call me Oscar." Osas gets to his feet. "Enough. You don keep Oscar here anymore."

Pressing charges would mean pushing the police into launching an investigation, digging up dirt, painting a target on the middle of his forehead. Osas is not ready to commit suicide.

"If you insist on not opening a case, then you have to sign that you've waived your right to press charges," the detective says. "I tell you what, Omorogie; you wait here and think about whether or not to press charges while I go get your waiver forms."

Osas snorts at the police officer in response.

After what seems like an eternity, the police officer returns and places a document before him on the table. "You just have to sign there and there."

Osas picks up the pen and scrawls a nonsensical signature on the pages. "Can I go?"

"Jab," says detective Booysen. "Your funeral."

Wordlessly, Osas strides out of the room.

Moments later, Detective Jiba enters. "No charges pressed, huh?"

"Not this one," Booysen answers contemplative.

"We'll profile him, keep a lookout," Jiba says. "He's a new member of the Nigerian crime syndicate."

Ruth has always known that running a brothel requires some spiritual assistance. Even though she was a woman from a taboo world, she was not arrogant enough to think that all her efforts in building the business were possible without any spiritual help.

She had heard of other brothel owners who consulted *sangomas*, traditional healers who help strengthen their businesses. She was willing to pay any price to have her business survive. Indeed, in her line of work, one is bound to make enemies, and physical protection is not always enough. Since she could not afford to bring down someone from her country and knew that Papi could not be persuaded to spend that much money on her no matter how well they pleasured each other between the sheets, she had to act on her own. Part of her wanted to keep an air of mystery alive among her girls about her unbreakable and flourishing success. But there was another side to her that felt a particular concern because she was not growing any younger, and her curiosity for the future got the better of her.

"I'll be right back," she said as she trotted by Esther and Ese.

"And where is the madam going," Esther said, looking at Ese and then back at Ruth.

"You must learn to mind your own. You have a big mouth these days, Esther," She said.

Esther sucked her teeth in as Ese laughed at her attitude being called to order by Ruth.

"You talk too much," Ese said.

"I will give you one slap, you goat," she said exasperated and marched off, leaving Ese laughing by herself.

Ruth hailed a taxi on Bree Street. The people in the taxi watched silently with obvious disapproval as she hopped in. Her sunglasses and hat filled the claustrophobic vehicle as she confidently claimed her seat.

The women behind her laughed mockingly as she pulled out her wallet.

"They do think it's there, "one young woman said to the other.

"They can only dream, "the other young woman replied.

Little did they know about her. Little did they know that no one should speak ill of people like her because fate weaves its thread, and one day you may end up at Emerald Escorts, like so many women in the country who once thought they had it good. She knows them all and women like Ruth do not forget even the slightest inflexion of voices. One day you will meet her on the street, and you will pay a huge prize.

She jumps off at MTN taxi rank and takes another taxi to Soweto. Taking out her mobile phone, she makes a call.

"Vilakazi... okay...address..." she speaks unabashedly in her Nigerian accent.

She jumps off at Vilakazi Street and makes her way to a two-room brick house. She opens the rusted squeaking gate, closes it softly and makes her way through the passage that leads to the backyard. She knocks on the door of the backroom and a gruff voice of a woman in *sangoma* attire—beads, goatskin band on her wrist—appears on the doorway.

"*Ngena*. Come inside,"she says, not offering the warmest welcome.

Ruth enters and slowly sits on the small bench, trying her best to be as comfortable as she possibly could.

"Please remove those heels," the woman commands.

Ruth removes her heels and places them by the doorway.

"Mamu Zodwa,"she says, greeting the woman.

"Yes, Ruth. I have been expecting you," she says, sniffing at the burning herb from her calabash.

"I wanted to know what I need to do to make my business survive."

"Women like you are always so interesting to me. You give half your souls away and expect all that you have to last forever, "the woman says, making strange ancestral noises.

"I did not come here to be judged, "Ruth snaps but quickly composes herself and speaks gently. "I just want to know what the future holds for me and my business. I have been having very strange dreams of a girl burning down my business."

Mam'Zodwa reaches out to take her traditional bag and spills out its contents of bones and divining elements. She continues to make peculiar ancestral voices.

"There is a girl. Beautiful. Very beautiful like a goddess of the waters but she will bring you to your ruin. She will bring everything you have worked for down. She will bring a child that will take everything away from you. "She launches again into ancestral voices.

"Whose child is it?" Ruth asks urgently.

"That I cannot say," the woman responds.

Ruth takes out a ball of money and lays it down to the *sangomas*.

The woman looks at the money, takes it, and informs Ruth who the father of the baby is, but does not identify the woman.

"I need to know who it is," she insists.

"They do not want to reveal it as yet. But you will know soon."

"Then you will help with this right now. That is a lot of money next to you. You will help me fix this problem, "Ruth demands."

As the *sangoma* prepares *muthi* for Ruth, she sits wondering who this woman will be. Could it be that she will bring *herself* to ruin? She is after all the only one sleeping with Osas. She needs an answer now.

"Take this and put it in a cup of tea. It will get rid of the child," Mam'Zodwa says. "Your future will continue to grow and grow once you have gotten rid of the child."

"You sure it this will work?" she asks.

"Yes. It has worked for many others. You can't even taste it," she says.

Ruth takes the *muthi* and walks backwards as she exits the backroom. She puts on her heels, walks towards the rusted squeaking gate, and leaves Soweto to go back to Braamfontein.

Success comes at a high cost, and for them, sacrifices are meant to be made even if that means shedding some blood along the way. Ruth feels no remorse. To feel compassion is to be weak.

Rubbing his head, Osas steps out of the police station into the bright light of day. To his left, Mboma and Kunta have been waiting for him to come out. He makes eye contact with them, unsettled by their stern gazes, full of unspoken threats.

"You! You alweady pay. But now you stay off our side of ze field," Kunta warns him.

Osas, ever defiant, but nervous without wanting to show it, gives them the middle finger. He will never let these dogs see the fear in him.

Mboma makes to go after Osas, but Kunta holds him back and smiles. "Next time, puisee."

Osas scoffs. "E be like una wan die!" He crosses the street and turns a corner even as the gangsters watch him—a target marked for an early entry into the land of the dead.

GANG DREAD

Osas knows that Papi will be in the office, but when he is buzzed into the room, he is surprised to see Ruth standing by the big man like an unwavering shadow. Ruth gasps when she sees how battered Osas is.

Papi, who is closing a briefcase, looks inquisitively at him. "Wetin you say happen to you?"

Osas knows that he will need to tell Papi what has happened and hesitates. "Na three guys wey dey talk French. Dem brush me for behind Domenico piazza side."

Papi stops, his eyes widen, and he stares at Osas for a minute. "The Francophone gang. Chike no tell you say na their area be that?"

"Na there I see market sell," Osas tries to explain.

Papi continues giving him a long hard stare. "Oya give me the money wey dey your hand."

Osas does not move a muscle but lowers his eyes to the plush carpet. "The French boys collect everything."

"You say?"

"Them take everything, boss," he repeats softly.

Papi does not burst into the rage he expects, which surprises Osas. Instead, he says, "You sabi say your this week rent dey inside there? I go allow Chike do you as him like." He snaps the briefcase shut and hands it to Osas. "Carry go down for me."

Briefcase in hand, Osas leaves Papi's office without another word and goes down to wait in the car park. Rubbing his head while he waits, Osas imagines what he would like to do to those Francophone beasts if they ever cross paths.

Papi and Ruth step out of the building and head towards Osas waiting by Papi's gold Mercedes Benz. Ruth leans in and kisses Papi on the cheek when they get to the vehicle. "Later, Don Papi," she says.

Papi nods at her, unlocks the door and climbs heavily into the driver's seat.

Ruth touches Osas lightly on the arm. Their eyes meet, but they do not say anything and Osas is suddenly confused. She removes her hand, then turns and walks away. Osas watches her for a moment before carefully placing the briefcase in the backseat. He walks around the vehicle to Papi's window as the ignition is turned on.

Papi regards him shortly. "Nna, number one: treat yourself. Number two: double your hustle, you dey owe me plenty money. Number three: start to find where you go sleep because I no dey pay Chike for your rent next week."

"Yes, boss," Osas says meekly.

Papi slides the automatic into place without another word and drives towards the parking lot exit where he turns east.

Osas returns sullen to the entrance of the building and is surprised to see Ruth waiting for him in the corridor.

"Make I see your face," Ruth says, inspecting the bruises without waiting for a response. He winces when she touches the bump above his left eye. "Follow me come my side make I clean you up," she says softly, holding his hand and inspecting the grazes on them.

Osas shakes his head. "Your hotel too far, I no go get train come back."

"No be my hotel we dey go," she replies. "My house no far."

The atmosphere at the KY barbershop is far from its usual. The shop is closed and there are no customers. The establishment is deserted, save for two Nigerians loitering as they talk outside, occasionally peeking through the window at the large-screen television mounted to the wall. They are interested in checking the scores of the ongoing muted football game on the TV.

In the inner room of the salon, which is out of bounds to all but Papi's inner circle, Kayode, Maskotoe and Chike sit close together counting money. The moment Kayode is done counting; he pockets the wad of money in his hand and glances at the open laptop on a nearby stool. He nods approvingly. "E sure."

Maskotoe finishes his own count, but a deep frown is set on his large square-jawed face. "Chike, how far nah? Three thousand six dey short."

Chike is puzzled. "How much dey there?"

"Eleven-four."

Chike scoffs. "Na complete be that."

"No be here we dey calculate am?"

"My friends no agree for una price," he tells him. "And full truck of stolen goods for night without receipt mean say I gats bribe police for road. Why you dey do like say you just dey come? Nna, chook your money for pocket, abeg."

Maskotoe slips his cut into his pocket, grumbling. "Abeg dey calculate everything from beginning. I no like make money short from wetin I dey expect."

There is a moment of silence before Kayode says, "Una don hear the latest from Naija?"

The two stare at him.

"E be like war go soon set with Buccaneers oh," Kayode goes on. "One of their men slap Aiye point, one girlfriend, for party."

"When this one happen?" Maskotoe enquires, intrigued by the news.

"Last night. Na Ruff Coin just dey give me the hands for Facebook now. Them go decide whether to knack de guy or na to warn am after this night meeting."

Chike is thoughtful for a moment. "Make we see. I no need tell una to watch una back. Buccaneer when dey here don dey find anything to take start fight."

"Make them just start," Kayode says. "Olorun, people go collect. This one no be that 2014 matter o—"

His words are cut short by the ring of the

doorbell to the barbershop. Maskotoe rises to his feet and heads to the door to take a look. He returns to inform Chike that the caller is for him. Chike slips out of the room and into the saloon to see Chamai standing just outside the barbershop door.

He beckons Chamai inside. "Chamai! Wetin dey happen na?"

Chamai looks at him, but it seems like his mind is elsewhere.

"So you got something for me?" Chike asks.

Chamai reaches into his pocket and brings out a thin roll of notes. He hands it over to Chike.

Chike grins as he takes the money and feeds it into his wallet. "Wasn't that ugly, heh?"

"I can't look myself in the mirror," Chamai replies flatly.

"No worry, you get used to it."

"I just need to raise my school fees."

"Definitely," Chike agrees. "I don arrange another client sharp sharp." He produces a scrap of paper from his back pocket on which an address is scrawled. He extends it to Chamai. "Get in and get out. Another easy picking."

Chamai glances at the paper, then at Chike. He looks at Chike like a mouse afraid of the cat, but he takes the piece of paper anyways. "When?"

"Eight o'clock this night. And no wear that your pullover go there o. Find something sexy."

He winks, taking out a hundred rand from his wallet and handing it to Chamai. But Chamai has no time for his humour and does nothing to hide it. You do not laugh at jokes when you feel you are the punch-line.

8

TAINTED SPIRITS

Osas groans as Ruth wipes his face with a towel soaked in hot water and antiseptic. His whole body hurts in so many places. They are on the couch in her sitting room. Despite his pains, Osas is amazed at the impressive decor and immaculate arrangement of the apartment. The air is laden with a fragrance. From the living room, you can hear vehicles zooming by the highway, their lights sending flashes onto a spot on the wall that is otherwise dimly lit by a lamp in a corner.

"So how long you live in the village?" she asks, wringing the towel and letting drops of water fall into the bowl on the coffee table.

"My whole life," he says solemnly. "I spent the past few months in Lagos and here."

"Lagos. Hmm. That crazy place," she says. "Any plans to go back?"

"For what?"

"Parents?"

Osas takes a deep breath. "No parents."

"They died?" she asks without emotion, as though asking him the colour of the floor.

"You too dey ask question," he says.

Ruth smiles. "You too dey form hard man, young guy like you. But I like am, *sha*." She leans closer. "I like you."

She rinses the towel in the bowl again and hands it to Osas, looking him in the eye. "Hold am, I dey come." She rises to her feet.

"Where?"

"Make I bring ice come," she says, disappearing into the bedroom.

Osas drops the towel on the table, pulls himself up and allows his attention to be drawn to the framed photographs on the wall. Stepping towards them, he inspects each one and finds himself stopping at a particular picture of a woman seated on a wall in a garden, dressed in black and white. He stares at it, his brows narrowing. There is something familiar, something—

"You like it?"

Osas spins around, startled. He had not heard her enter. She is changed from the woman who had only excused herself moments ago, this time dressed in panties and bra under an open cream satin house robe. He blinks anxiously, swallowing hard.

She closes the space between them and places an ice pack onto his forehead. "Abi you prefer flesh and blood wey dey here?"

"I ... wetin you ..." he breathes, stupidly choking on his words.

"I wan fuck you," she tells him.

Osas feels everything spinning out of control. This is Papi's woman. The whole thing is just unthinkable. Touching her amounted to something grievous. Something unmentionable. Treasonous, even. It sure would earn him a bullet in the head. She kisses his parted lips softly. Her hand snakes down to his crotch. She seems to know where his balls are, and she applies some light pressure there. He has never known such a touch in all his life. She seems to know how to go about flicking every switch he did not imagine existed in his body. Her tongue plays around his lips and glides into their parting.

At this point, Osas stops thinking.

Chamai's eyes are shut tight. He is kneeling on the centre of a large hardwood board in a storeroom dimly lit by a shaded red light. All he is wearing is a G-string. His arms are bound together, with the rope looped through a bolt in the wall at the head of the board. A mask covers his face. Underneath the mask, he is gagged with a ball gag.

The tall pink man with a peculiar foreign accent had started very kindly and friendly. He had said he would give Chamai an extra two thousand rand if they could, "Just have a bit of fun and play a few different characters from the movies together. That's all I want to do," he had said. "I'm just bored."

He told Chamai his name was Aniken but changed the topic when Chamai asked him where he was from. He had offered Chamai a whiskey in the seedy hotel room they had been. They had talked for a bit, Chamai sipping on his drink and trying to answer the man's questions about himself, keep up with his strange conversation, peppered with words and expressions he did not understand. Aniken had said he found the room too depressing and asked if they could go through to his office, where he could show Chamai the work he did. The man had said he might even be able to give Chamai a job. Chamai had gone along, thinking that with this man, his luck might finally have changed.

When they arrived at the man's office in an industrial part of town Chamai has never known, there was no signage outside. The man had shown Chamai in and seated himself behind a small desk, explaining that his floor of the building was being renovated. They had another round of drinks and then the man had asked Chamai to join him in sniffing the yellow-white powder he had brought out of a desk drawer. Chamai had declined at first. The man took out a thousand rand, handed it to him and said he would give him another thousand rands for each line he sniffed up his nose. It had been the first time Chamai had snorted cocaine and it worked. He felt on top of the world.

Now Chamai deeply regrets his decision to come here, to have snorted the cocaine. The man, Aniken, which Chamai now knows is not his real name, had taken out a big bag of costumes. It was fun at first. Chamai had dressed as a naval officer with regalia and all, while the man had dressed as a pirate with an eye patch. The man called the game 'The Flying Dutchmen' and they had thrown crumpled pieces of paper at one another, running around the spacious office, laughing. Then the man had suggested

'Django.' Chamai was to be a slave, while Aniken played a plantation owner. Chamai had gone along with it and even let the man tie up his hands. Then everything had turned. As soon as the man knew his arms were secure, he delivered a vicious punch to Chamai's face. Then the big man, far stronger than Chamai, had straddled him and forced the ball gag into his mouth. He had been dragged into the storeroom, where there was a camera on a tripod in the corner. As soon as Chamai saw the camera, he knew he had made the biggest mistake of his life.

The man is behind him, also wearing only a G-string, but instead of a devil's mask like the one that he had placed over Chamai's face, he wears a helmet with a dark visor.

He has a multi-strand whip is in his hand, and when the man strikes, Chamai whimpers into the ball gag in his mouth, his buttocks and upper thighs receiving a slash of painful welts. He wonders if he is bleeding. The man swings his whip again, and Chamai begins to cry, thinking he will swallow his tongue.

"Shut up, demon!" the man screams, his strange foreign accent stronger than ever. He goes over to the camera and pushes a button. Taking off his helmet, he crosses over to Chamai where he lifts the mask and unbuckles the ball gag. Chamai gasps and starts begging the man to stop. The man laughs at him. It is the laugher of one enjoying a game.

"I think screaming will be better," he whispers into Chamai's ear, pulling the mask back down over his face.

Chamai begs. "Stop! Please! Please stop!"

But the man ignores him and goes over to a counter behind the camera where Chamai hears him take a long sniff. He then puts his helmet back on and pushes the record button on the camera. He picks up the whip again. "Shut up demon!" he shouts, and then the lashes are repeated on Chamai's buttocks and across the backs of his thighs. Chamai howls in pain but is silenced with another slash of the whip that takes the breath out of him.

The man suddenly moves closer, pulls aside the G-string and plunges his erect penis viciously into Chamai. Chamai cries, tears rolling freely down his cheeks. He wriggles and grunts, but the man just keeps going, thrusting, moaning, and spanking Chamai across his buttocks. Then he climaxes with a deep, exasperated breath, finally pulling himself out. Chamai tries to catch his breath. He thinks of a way to break free, when all of a sudden, he feels something cold being applied to his anus.

"No-no-no, stop, stop, stop," Chamai begs but it is too late. Pain like nothing he has ever felt in his life suddenly shoots through him as the man begins inserting a large object into Chamai's anus. Sweat begins pouring down his face and mucus and spittle flow freely from his mouth and nose as he feels his skin tear and the man begins to force the object viciously in and out of him, again and again.

Chamai passes out.

When Chamai wakes up, he spasms in shock. The man is seated on a chair nearby, still wearing the helmet and looking down on him. Chamai's eyes widen in horror, but he cannot move because of the pain. He is lying on the floor, in his blood. His hands are still bound, but he has been loosened from the bolt on the wall. He feels his feet have been freed too.

The man takes off his helmet. "Hush, hush. There's a good boy," he says, drawing close and stroking Chamai's arm.

Chamai lays dead still, eyes closed, taking deep breaths and groaning monotonously. The man sprawls himself on the floor beside Chamai.

"That was for them," he whispers into Chamai's ear. "This is for me now." For a long while, the man just lies there next to him, staring at his face. Chamai has the feeling that this man, whoever he is, is sure to kill him. At this stage, he wants just that. He wants it to be quick—for all the pain, he felt to come to a swift end. He is furious at the world and at this freak trying to get some sort of twisted affection from him.

The man sits up and goes over to the table behind the camera. He takes another long sniff. When he comes back, he picks up the helmet and leans over to whisper into Chamai's ear.

"It's okay. Everything is going to…"

Chamai moves unexpectedly and sinks his teeth hard into the man's neck with all the strength he can muster. The man screams but cannot wrestle himself free. Chamai lets go and spits out the flesh in his mouth. The man staggers back against the wall, clutching his bleeding neck. His eyes shine with wild disbelief at Chamai, and then it begins to mellow. A smile plays on his face. It lingers on even as the life drains from his eyes. He slides against the wall and then, like a rag doll, he comes to rest on the floor and goes limp.

Chamai begins to cry, long and painful sobs that wrack his entire body.

Every part of his body, within and without, hurts. He winces and groans, then painfully manages to get up on his feet. Walking with awkward and unsteady steps, he moves about the store and rummages around. On a desk, he finds a cigarette lighter. It is an awkward task, and his hands are unsteady, but he burns away a portion of the rope with which his hands are bound. He manages the task without burning his flesh, but the whole stores smells badly of burnt jute.

A door somewhere in the corner is slightly ajar. It appears to lead into a bathroom. He heads towards it. His guess is right, for sure enough it is a small bathroom, surprisingly well kept. He washes his face, hands, and tries as best as he can to clean up some of the blood on his legs, but the area around his anus is too sensitive to touch. He hobbles out to the office and, with great difficulty, begins to dress. When he is finished, he opens the desk drawer where he had earlier seen the man take money out, and pockets all the cash he finds. Chamai then makes his way out through the front door and into a sunlit Sunday morning. He is no longer Chamai. Chamai has died inside that storeroom.

Ruth and Osas are under the sheets, exhausted from their lovemaking. He lets her trace aimless patterns on his bare chest, enjoying the sensations of her fingers.

"Your name suppose be 'small but mighty,'" she says. "See as body dey do me. Old woman like me."

Osas chuckles. "Wetin you go come talk if I settle down handle you?"

She smiles and runs her fingers down to his groin. "I no need tell you say this matter na between us. Papi fit kill you if him find out."

He says nothing. Papi had not crossed his mind since Ruth had begun touching him, sending him to unimaginable planes of pleasure. She is better than April is, he thought to himself.

"You get girlfriend for Naija?" she asks, startling him with her question.

"Nah." He thinks of Oghogho.

"Here nko?"

"No."

"You sure?"

"I no dey do love," he replies, and his own response surprises him. "Na hustle I come."

She grins. "Hustle sha no dey stop konji. Na why my business dey move."

At that moment, a message comes through on Osas' phone on the bedside table. He reaches for it. The message is from Andre, written in capital letters: SUP? WHERE HAVE YOU BEEN? CALL ME!!!

Alarmed, he jumps out of the bed and starts dressing.

Ruth is confused. "Wetin happen? Where you dey go?"

"As hustle no dey stop konji, konji sef no dey stop hustle," he replies wittily.

She smiles. "You be proper Ishan boy."

Andre is irritated when Osas hurries into the Burger King.

"Sorry I dey late," Osas apologises, sitting down opposite his host. "I dey come from across town."

"Exactly. You have been too busy lately. I haven't seen you in how many, two weeks?"

"Haba! E never tay like that, but I call you last weekend. Na your machine I get."

"Yeah. I flew out to Paris for a few days."

Osas beams. "So wetin you bring come?"

Andre chuckles, irritated but amused. "Wetin I bring come? You Nigerians will be the death of me. Always asking for stuff."

Osas frowns. "Person no fit follow you play again?"

"I know. Besides, I am more interested in what you have got for me. Got that legit yayo for a brother?"

Osas clears his throat. "No, not today. In couple of days. Them rob me. My boss travel. E get as tings be right now, but I go soon arrange."

Andre stares at him, unimpressed. "I don't have a couple of days, bru."

Osas feels the tension rising. "Okay, give me two hours. Make I make some calls for you."

Andre shakes his head, upset. "I need my shit right now. I cannot tell the models 'a few days.' You know what; I know where to go. See you later, Oscar." He rises abruptly. "I'll text you," he says, then heads for the exit and out into the night.

Andre detests this bar. It is too far off the track for his liking. The surrounding buildings are all dilapidated and filled with drug addicts and homeless people. He never feels safe coming here, to this sneaky place where shady business transactions from people like him are too damned obvious. A handful of people are at the bar, drinking and arguing loudly in French. Some are at the pool table in the corner; others sit silently at rickety tables. Andre knows where he is going, knows the people he is looking for.

"Good Lawd!" comes the thick French accent. "If it not Andre, come back fwom ze dead, huh?" A voice hails him from a booth in the darkness at the back of the bar.

Even before he turns, Andre recognises the voice. It is Kunta. He goes to the corner, smiling bravely, where the Francophone gangsters–Mboma, Omoro, Kunta, and two others sit – faces veiled in darkness, smoke emanating from their cigarettes, watching him.

Andre tries to adjust his eyes to the poor lighting.

"Where gav yoo bin, man?" Kunta asks.

"Here and there," Andre replies tactfully. "Work, y'know."

"Yip," Kunta says, disbelieving. "And how has zat bin?

"Good. Not bad, y'know? Just very busy."

Mbomo asks, "Yoo want fix?"

Andre beams. "Exactly."

"Alight. Meet Omoro in zer bafwoom, how much yoo want?"

"I need six Andre says, and then adds, "But it has to be good. My clients are high end. They do not want the shit stuff. They're willing to pay more for quality."

"OK. Go-go, Omoro will bwing it."

Inside the bar's filthy toilet, Andre waits nervously. He feels trapped in here. He knows that instead of bringing him what he needs they could just as well bring him a body bag. Finally, the big Omoro steps into the bathroom and walks over to the urinal, forcing Andre to wait and listen. When he is finished, he comes over to Andre at the basin and washes his hands, not taking his eyes off him on the mirror. "Tree tousand," the big man says.

"That's a little expensive, isn't it?"

"Is good," Omoro, says simply.

Andre takes the money from out of his wallet and counts out three thousand. It is more than he had expected to pay—he will be a bit short now—but he is not about to start arguing. Andre exchanges it for the plastic wrap containing the balls of cocaine.

"Thanks man. I just want to test the quality first," he says, going into one of the cubicles. Once inside, he quickly undoes the wrapping of one of the balls, wipes the toilet's lid with his sleeve, and then flicks some of the cocaine out on it. He then ties the packet up expertly again to avoid any difference to the others. Taking out a note from his wallet, he rolls it, and then sniffs the powder on the porcelain surface. He stops for a moment, sniffing. That is good, he decides. Good enough for sure.

Exiting the bathroom, he stops at the end of the corridor, listening to the conversation taking place in French between the other gang members. After hearing what has been said, he wants to get out of this place now.

As Andre is about to walk through the bar to leave, Kunta stops him with a hand on his shoulder menacingly. "And don be a l'etranger, huh," the gangster says.

Andre chuckles nervously. "I won't, don't worry," he says, and then heads for the exit, a little too quickly.

In his semi-dark apartment, Chamai sits, engulfed in shame. He clenches his hair with his sweaty palms. His heart feels full of the betrayals. Breath in a turmoil, he stands up finally, and goes to the kitchen sink half-bent, as though he wants to vomit all the sins branded on him by Johannesburg.

All for the money. All for the filth of men who spoke proudly of the devil's work, of men who boasted of the disgusting pleasures of the world. He knew he was on this world but not of it. His humanity had always been an unusual illustration for those to be condemned. Moving away from the kitchen and onto his mattress, he looks up at the ceiling.

"What has he made me into?" He ponders, teary-eyed as the lights of the city pierce through the lace curtains, casting a dumb shadow of his body on the walls. He stares into it as if the power to give it life was ordained in his eyes.

"Maybe..." he whispers. "Maybe if I did not agree. What am I? Who am I...?" His thought runs wild but is suddenly interrupted by a notification on his phone. He picks it up to read the text. Nothing special. He puts it aside for a moment, and then picks it up again. Scrolls to his mobile internet browser and searches for pornographic images to make him feel like himself again. Like a man. He wants to feel what it feels like to be a man.

He watches, with undisturbed attention, as voluptuous women are dragged into drab hotel rooms, penetrated by well-endowed men, moaning in false pleasure. His hand makes his way into his pants and manoeuvres his manhood. He unbuttons his pants, pulls down his underwear and vigorously masturbates to the moans and groans, the smacked buttocks and sweaty coitus of people, who for a moment could make him remember he is indeed a man.

"Ah," he whimpers as he comes, curling his toes in ecstasy. He takes a deep breath and releases it with a piece of his spirit, giving off to strangers of sexual fantasy. He pulls up his pants and continues to stare at his shadow.

"These people are disgusting," he speaks to the dumb shadow on the walls.

"I should have gone more often to church. I should have tried harder to find a girl. I should have..." he pauses. He then scrolls through the sites of sexual wonderland studiously again as if something had caught his attention.

"Gay porn..." he reads out loud. "Maybe this is where that pig gets his ideas from."

He sits up and watches. He closes his phone and thinks fast as if some tsunami of an idea is about to drown him even deeper into his resentment.

He picks up his phone again and downloads a dating app. He waits patiently as he anticipates the successful installation. He thinks and then registers his profile on Grindr.

"Largest social networking app for gay, bi, trans and queer people," he reads, disgusted, with a deep-seated hatred for what they thought he was. He rummages through his phone's gallery and chooses his Sunday-best picture he could find.

At the back of his mind, he knows what he is doing does not speak to his already tainted spirit. He knows what is impending, growing in his mind, is not who he is but what he has become.

Folding his arms and unfolding them again, he must get this feeling out somehow. He must channel this anger, the resentment and immorality, on something or someone. As his rage and anger grow, so does his guilt. He gently shakes his head and sells himself to his self-created darkness. He comes up with a plan.

"I just want them dead," he thinks viciously. He stands and paces up and down. First message.

"Show me your dick," it reads.

He is taken aback.

"Show me yours," he replies.

The exchange goes on for about an hour as pictures of selfies and private parts between the two fly around.

And there it is! The idea to release all his pain. To kill what Chike had made him be. All these godless people and all these sinners. His eyes widened vehemently as this was the only way, the only way, because if God would allow such a thing to happen to him, then it is clear He does not care for him. And if He did not care for him, then he will assume vengeance on a stranger whom He has made in the image and likeness of Him.

"Meet up," a message flashes. He types back without thinking and agrees to meet someone who has done him wrong.

"Tell me where and when."

"Jamz. You know it," the message asked.

"Yes, I do," he types, blood rushing to his head, his shadow looking down at him as if it has grown a face, smiling malevolently at him and coaxing him to do the unthinkable.

Three days later, in the evening, Chimai is in a scrambled but confident mood, his face unsmiling. He cleans himself up and dons on his best attire, covered by a hoodie from his closet, and makes his way out of his apartment.

Walking down the night street, he is full of nerves but determined to meet his victim, to lure him into his repugnant plan.

He reaches Jamz and waits outside for a moment. He looks deep into the entrance and is about to seal his fate; take a life, as was his taken from him.

"Still coming," a message lands into his inbox.

"Just outside."

"Okay. Wearing a white top. Short fade. Light skin." The message lights up as Chamai walks, overwhelmed and ambushed by darkness he has not faced before. As he enters the building, April walks out, brushing past him.

"Sorry," she says as she continues to make her way onto the street.

He looks at her, then turns back and enters. The young man, prissy and prim, sees him and waves in the romantic manner of black and white movies. He stands still as a statue. The young man smiles, cute but ignorant of a raging homophobe meeting an unsuspecting prey.

"It's me, Thabo," the young man beckons to join him. Chamai stands still, his hands shaking, sweat falling into his shirt, mouth dry like the desert of his mind.

He steps back and quickly walks out. Chamai walks outside onto the street, the back of his hand on his mouth.

Osas walks up the deserted street to the entrance of Chike's apartment block. He stiffens on seeing April, huddled in a corner. She looks up and, as he approaches, straightens. Osas draws close, and by the headlamps of a passing car, he notices her swollen cheeks, the black eye, the dried mascara-stained tears.

"Wetin happen to you?" he asks.

April's eyes glisten, but she says nothing.

"You and pesin follow fight?"

"Na customer." Her voice is a croak. She casts her head downwards.

Osas sighs, pulls her into a hug. She shudders and begins sobbing. "Hey, no dey cry abeg. You go dey, alright."

She sniffs. "Abeg make I follow you sleep," she pleads, breaking the embrace. "Abeg. I no fit go back de this night."

He is instantly wary. "Chike fit come back. You don tell Madam Ruth?"

"Na she carry the man give me."

Osas scratches his head.

She is looking into his eyes in desperation. "Osas, I take God name beg you."

He cannot take her in; Chike will turn into a crazy bull if he returns to see a whore in his apartment. However, Osas cannot bring himself to leave her out here either, alone, a potential prey on a night filled with nothing but awful prospects. He takes a deep breath, and then says, "Follow me."

At the same time that Osas is leading April into the building, Chike is inside a coffee shop, alone in a corner, sipping on a cup of tea and staring unflinchingly in the direction of a couple at another table. He is not seeing the woman in the red dress; it is the handsome man he is watching. He stares longingly.

A rattled-looking Chamai appears in front of him.

"My man!" Chike hails excitedly, "Sit down."

"No. I'll stand," Chamai says flatly. He has a strange look on his face that Chike cannot help but notice.

Chike looks at him questioningly. "You dey okay?"

Chamai takes out a thin roll of notes from his pocket and gives it to Chike.

Chike counts the money and pockets it, smiling satisfactorily. "Chamai, you see wetin I tell you? This thing na piece of cake. Basically, na free money."

Chamai gives him a hard stare.

Chike continues nevertheless. "Well, almost free." He brings out a slip of paper from his back pocket. "You sabi wetin I mean, sha." He slides the paper across the table to Osas. "Na our next payday be that."

Chamai reaches for the paper, but instead of picking it up, he slowly and deliberately pushes it back. Chike blinks, confused.

"I'm done," Chamai says, with the finality of a man on the edge.

"You wan take break today?"

"I am done. Forever."

Chike clears his throat, adjusts himself uneasily in his chair. "I no know say small money dey belleful you."

"This is not about the money. I can't do this anymore."

"You sure say you know wetin you dey do?" he asks, amused.

"I don't fucking know what I'm doing!" Chamai shouts, his eyes darkening. "That's why I have to stop right now!"

Chike stands up to shush him, but the exasperated Chamai flings his hand away. "Stay away from me!"

The patrons in the coffee shop all turn to look in their direction. Chike swallows hard, unsure of how best to handle the situation. Chamai storms out. Chike sits down again and considers what to do when his phone begins to ring. He picks it up.

"Madam Ruth, how far nah?" he asks, feigning normalcy. "I dey. See, make we talk later abeg."

Chike ends the call without waiting for a response. He thinks of Chamai and grinds his teeth. Something will have to be done about this. Scrolling through his phone's contact list, he finds who he is looking for. He dials the number and listens impatiently as the line buzzes. Finally, a click.

"Osas, how far? I won return to the apartment tonight, but here's the thing, I want make you pack up out of there first thing tomorrow morning." The ultimatum has been delivered. He ends the call.

The eviction order makes him feel better.

9

SUICIDE PACT

Osas has just finished packing a travelling bag and is dragging it to the door when it swings open.

Chike stands in the jamb with some wide-eyed, poorly dressed and skinny teenage boy in tow.

"I been think say you go don comot by now," Chike growls.

"Chyko, abeg give me one week make I use know where I go enter," Osas pleads.

Chike shakes his head. "You don do pass one month for street. You suppose know your way."

"Just one week, abeg."

"That kind time no dey, my guy. Shebi you see say I get new guest. Three of us no fit stay here."

Osas nods in suppressed anguish.

"I for even reason you," Chike goes on, "but nothing pain me pass those women wey you dey carry come my house even when I warn you. If I no take time, na so you go drag police come."

Osas says nothing. He pulls the bag along dejectedly as he goes out.

Osas remembers when a certain Chief Nosakhare invited him to his house.

"I have an important job for you and your friends to do for me," Chief Nosakhare had said, sitting in his car, with Osas beside him. "I need you guys to go to that EFCC office on High Court Road and get my two boys out. I will give you the picture of the EFCC Officer that went and picked them from their house. You will kill him. His family is in Jos. I will arrange for people in Plateau that will kill his wife and children this weekend."

Osas was shocked, with his mouth open.

Chief Nosakhare continued speaking. "If you can't get the boys out, burn down the place at night. I am offering you 2.5 million."

Osas could see how angry this man was so he decided not to talk, but listen.

"My boys did nothing," Chief Nosakhare kept speaking to Osas, without looking at him. "I have gone there to speak to the Zonal Head. The man said he wants 8 million. Right now, I do not have that kind of money, and I do not want them to charge the boys to a cult. The Zonal Head cannot give me the name of the petitioner. They know I would have killed whoever gave my boys' name to that bastard agency."

Osas turned to him now.

"I have a suggestion," he said in a meek voice. "I want to suggest that we find one of the officers on the team, kill him and keep a suicide note. This will send a signal to the Zonal Head and the officer leading the team."

Chief Nosakhare thought for a while and said sharply, "Get your friends together. Do anything to get my boys out ASAP before they charge them to court."

Osas stepped out of the car and banged the door shut.

Two days later, there was a report in *The Punch* newspaper. Chief Nosakhare read it in his veranda.

EFCC operative dies of suspected suicide, police await autopsy

Published September 7, 2019

Eniola Akinkuotu, Abuja

The Edo State Police Command has commenced an investigation into the death of an operative of the Economic and Financial Crimes Commission in Benin, the Edo State capital.

Although investigations have not been concluded, it is suspected that the deceased, Williams Oyibogare, died of suicide because two bottles of a pesticide, Sniper, were found in his home located at the Giwa Amu area along the Airport Road.

It was further alleged that a suicide note was found on his phone, which the police have already recovered.

The Spokesman for the EFCC, Mr Wilson Uwujaren, confirmed Oyibogare's death but said the commission was waiting for the police to conclude its investigation before making any further comment.

"It is true that one of our operatives died.

The police have begun an investigation into the matter, and we hope to hear from them soon. That is all we can say for now," Uwujaren said.

A colleague of the deceased told The Punch that Oyibogare recently returned from his annual leave looking emaciated.

She, however, said it was too soon to come to any conclusion.

"He returned from leave recently. He looked pale and seemed to have lost weight. He may have died from an illness, or it could also have been suicide, but we cannot say for sure since we do not live with him. Let us wait for the police to conclude its probe. An autopsy would be able to reveal the real cause of death," she said.

Speaking with our correspondent on the telephone, the Police Public Relations Officer, Edo Command Chidi Nwabuzor, said the police would wait for the autopsy before making further comment on the matter.

Nwabuzor said, "Investigations are ongoing, and it would be too soon to make any conclusions at this stage; it is too early to make any pronouncements. Of course, there will be an autopsy to know the cause of death and inquire about what happened."

As Chief Nosakhare read the article, he beamed. His phone rang. He looked at the screen to see that it was Osas.

"That's my boy," he said, then answered the call. "You did it, my boy."

Osas would tell Chike later that Chief Nosakhare paid him the money and he disappeared from Benin City the next day. However, he did not know about the EFCC official who had died by suicide. The Chief told him about it. But Osas did not kill the man. He was not going to tell the Chief anything. He needed the money, and once he had it, he headed to Lagos on a night bus.

For Chief Nosakhare, his visa racketeering business could not continue, because, after a week, the EFCC officials were at his house to arrest him. They barged into his home and searched everywhere while he stood in shock and handcuffs. They brought out hundreds of international passports with different names, which one of the officers sat down to read out loudly:

1. *Odeminlin Dyson Asuelimen*
2. *Okosun Akhator*
3. *Ihenyen Donatus Ehijie*

4. Imoni Anthonia Ogochukwu
5. Imoni Lucky Ehichioya
6. Akhogba Ebinehita Victor

He looked up at Chief Nosakhare and asked;"Where are these ones going to?"

Chief Nosakhare answered; sweat dripping all over his face: "Italy."

"How much did you charge them? And how do you get them?"

He was still shaking: "Dear Sir, they come to me. I do not go searching for them. Even before I talk, they pay money into my account."

"Seriously?"

"Yes, sir." He continued, "They beg me to help them with visa, so they can run away to Europe. They offer me a lot of money. From eight hundred thousand naira to a million naira for a Schengen, visa. All of them."

"So," the EFCC Officer continued, "these ones have paid?"

"Yes, sir," Chief Nosakhare said. "And when they pay and get their visa, they will still come and petition at EFCC that I am into visa racketeering. They are not good people."

The EFCC officials looked at each other. One of the officers holding Chief Nosakhare asked, "Do you have any cash at home?"

Chief Nosakhare nodded: "Yes, sir."

He began to remove the handcuff, before he said, "Bring the cash and we will leave you! How much do you have?"

Chief Nosakhare began to panic. "I have about six hundred thousand naira, sir."

They let him run into his bedroom, and he came out with black nylon of the cash he had saved under his bed. He handed it to them. They peeped into the nylon once, and then left with it.

Chief Nosakhare breathed in and out in short gasps. "Osas didn't do his job!"

When Chike heard this story from Osas, he laughed hard and said, "You Edo people love visa so much."

One of the people in the Nigerian restaurant— Grace Restaurant—a Yoruba man who sold herbal drinks, joined the conversation.

"Yes," he said. "An Edo man can kill you because of a visa."

"Why is it so?" Chike asked Osas.

"I don't know, baba," Osas frowned.

"If they don't get the visa they want, they will

either go and do juju or come after you with a gun,,"
the Yoruba man continued. "I had experiences, man.
Edo man, visa, and Italy are glued together."

It was after that experience, that Chief Nosakhare
left Nigeria, to South Africa.

Andre is at his usual plastic table at the Burger King
when Osas walks in with his travelling bag.

"Going somewhere?" he asks, as Osas sits down.

"My roommate chase me comot."

"Why?"

"He want space for him small brother wey him
carry come," Osas replies.

"Such a shame. So where are you going to put
up now?"

"I no know," he says, exasperated. "I just dey
street for now. Them steal my money and product
that I got payback for."

"C'mon you can't sleep in the street." Andre is
thoughtful for a moment. "You could stay at mine till
you sort yourself out."

Osas brightens up. "Talk true?"

"Sure."

"Thanks, baba. I appreciate."

Andre shrugs off his gratitude. He has his

reasons. "Thought you wanted us to have a burger, but let's get your bag to the apartment first. Come on, Oscar."

At the club, the music is particularly loud since it is a Saturday night. The disc jockey is in full swing, and the crowd is especially amped. Women are on the dance floor, making sultry moves with their bodies while the men try to get close, all between the colourful and pervasively flashing lights and thumping bass from concealed speakers.

Chike, in the company of the new teenager, has just joined a table where Kayode, Maskotoe, and the rest of the usual people are.

"How far, Chike?" Kayode asks, in greeting, and then gestures to Chike's companion. "Who be this one?"

"Na my new boy," he answers.

"You na sharp guy o," Kayode admonishes him. "Him just dey enter from Naija?"

"Na Guinea him from. Na here I meet am."

Kayode makes a funny face.

"Why you dey ask, abi you don join police?" Chike asks.

"I don dey see you with too many boys these days. I just wan know whether you don change team."

"Na your papa team I change to," Chike retorts.

Laughter erupts.

"Una dey laugh, abi? Like the idiot, no know say all na business."

"I no know oh," Kayode says, enjoying himself. "Your business too plenty."

Chike turns to the boy he has brought. "*Hey?*"

"Yeah," the boy says. "Wanna go toilet."

"Over there," Chike points.

The teenager hurries off through the crowd. Chike picks up a glass, dumps out its dregs, and then pours himself a drink from one of the Heineken quarts on the table. He swallows hard in a single gulp. On the dance floor, girls break into an excited shout as the DJ switches tracks and the tempo accelerates. Just then, Chike glances up and freezes. Steve is talking to his Guinean. He jumps to his feet and marches at them.

"Hey, hey, what the fuck?" he shouts, barely able to keep himself in check. He steps in between them, "Go back table. Right away!" he orders the boy before turning to Steve and poking him in the chest. "Wetin you think say you dey do?"

"Do I need permission to say hi?" Steve asks, drunk. "C'mon man, it's a free country, hey!"

"Carry your 'hi' go outside, you hear me so?" Chike warns. "Inside here na me dey run things."

"Bullshit!" Steve exclaims, pushing past Chike, and heading deeper into the club.

Maddened Chike strides past and blocks him. "Where you dey go? Comot outside now!"

Steve grabs Chike and shoves him aggressively out of his path. Chike staggers, crashing into the bodies of the people closest to him. Pulling himself straight, Chike charges at him. The first punch slams into Steve's nose, the second into the side of his neck, knocking him back to the floor. The big Maskotoe dashes over to restrain Chike.

Steve stands up, wiping his bloodied nose. "Think I'm one of your slaves?" he spits. "Fuck you man!"

"You don jonz, I go finish you!" Chike swears at him. Maskotoe holds him back from lunging again at Steve.

Three of the club bouncers hurry over. "You guys have to leave!" a giant of a man in a leather jacket brimming with muscles shouts at the two of them.

Chike and Steve simultaneously engage in verbal

protest as they are shepherded out of the club. As soon as they are outside Steve sidles away, wiping at his bloodied nose and swearing drunkenly into the night.

Chike takes out money from his wallet and tucks it into the security man's palm. "You know how it is, huh," he says, winking conspiratorially at them.

They laugh and let him back inside.

There is Thapelo Nkosi. He was originally from Durban but a student of the University of Western Cape. He lived in Cape Town before a Nigerian man broke his heart.

"Those Nigerians are uncultured and misogynistic, hey," he complained to a random woman he met at a bar on Long Street. "They are also dirty and noisy. They claim they are also endowed. This dude dumped me! He will never want to be seen in public with me, hey!" He said this and then took a sip from his glass of white wine.

The random woman looked at him and felt pity. She noted the number of times Thapelo threw in "literally" in any sentence. He told her he would head to Johannesburg next week. He said he was on a mission to destroy Nigerian men and ruin them.

"Don't let them hurt you," the random woman said. "I hear they are dangerous."

Thapelo sighed. "I know they are," he continued. "But that man dumped me, hey."

"How did you meet him?"

"On Grindr, hey," he said.

"Grindr?" she asked.

"It's a dating app for gay people."

She nodded her head and drank from her beer. "And?"

"He invited me over to his apartment," Thapelo said. "And we did it. After that, he would invite me over and give me some money. I visited him every day, but he would never take me out for lunch or anything, but he gave me loads of money."

"He is generous."

"Yes," he said. "That is why I literally feel bad. I have literally tried calling his number, it is not on and I have checked his apartment. I was told he does not live there anymore. He literally dumped me, hey."

The random woman was now irritated. She finished her beer and said to Thapelo. "It was nice meeting you. Good luck."

Thapelo stared as she retreated from the Long Street Cafe, where he continued to sip his wine and think about the Nigerian man, who dumped him.

Thapelo had a target. He had heard from other South African men and women who had dated Nigerians that they were flamboyant, extravagant and generous. He also heard they were good in bed. As a student, he would not mind a side hustle to take care of his financial needs at the university. So, getting a Nigerian would be his ultimate goal: someone who would satisfy his body, soul and, most importantly, his bank account. That was when he opened a profile on Grindr and spent weeks looking for Nigerians. He was lucky. He found one.

The Nigerian man was called Bola. He lived in De Waterkant Luxury Apartments. It was a beautifully decorated place. Whenever Thapelo went over for a night, he would not want to leave the next morning. He came with his rucksack because he would always find something to steal: unused perfumes, watches and face-wash.

Bola knew that Thapelo stole, but he did not bother saying anything. Bola had his plans, too. He was in Cape Town for a deal. As soon as it fell into place, he would be on the next flight to Lagos where his fiancé waited to be wed. He needed a lot of money for his Yoruba traditional wedding and owambe. While Thapelo was planning in his head to spend the rest of his life with Bola, Bola was plotting about how to vamoose Mzansi once his money was cleared. For him, Thapelo was no different from a tool he would use to masturbate. He did not attach any sentiment to their meetups. Seriously, they met online. You did not marry someone who you had met online. Moreover, Bola never had it in mind to marry a man. "*Olorun maje,*" he would say to himself, standing in front of a mirror. "God forbid! How can I marry a man?"

One night, Thapelo did what Bola said young South Africans do—emotionally blackmail Nigerians. He read out tweets from a South African man to Bola.

Katlego Masupa
@katlego_masupa

Can we all agree that Nigerian men are?

17:50 - 18/05/2020 Twitter for iPhone
41 Retweets 131 Likes

There was a liturgy of responses, calling Nigerian men all sorts of names. As Thapelo read the comments, Bola dozed off. When Thapelo looked his way and saw that he was snoring, disappointment clambered into his heart.

It was in the middle of the night that, Bola woke up and moved his hands into Thapelo's clothes. Bola fumbled with his penis, and his ass, which he murmured was soft, and slowly began to finger him. Thapelo, the South African boy, began to moan and groan for Bola, the Nigerian boy. He moaned and began to sweat in the middle of the night. The creaking of the bed followed. As was Bola worried his next-door neighbour might hear the sounds, he carried Thapelo into the sitting room, put the TV on at its loudest, and began to tear Thapelo apart.

Thapelo might agree with anyone on anything they said against Nigerians, but he would say to himself, "They are literally good in bed."

Only if Thapelo knew what Bola thought of him. Bola would never let his fellow Nigerians who visited him even see a shadow of Thapelo. He only invited Thapelo on the nights he had no Nigerian visiting him. If they saw Thapelo, they would raise an alarm. Thapelo was effeminate and loved walking around in bum shorts that highlighted his big ass.

"All South African men have big asses more than their women. Especially those Zulu boys," a Nigerian barber, who was cutting Bola's hair at Four Points, had said one day, and everyone burst into laughter. While the South Africans made fun of the Nigerians on Twitter, the Nigerians were busy, in their hair salons and electronic shops, making fun of South Africans.

You would hear them say, "Never make friends with these young South Africans because you begin to receive requests for e-wallet of R150."

Another Nigerian said, "And many of them don't know their fathers."

"That is why they do not respect anyone," another cut in, speaking in Pidgin. "South Africans never apologise for anything."

"Every child needs a father figure in their lives," Bola said. "And the young male South African thinks they can prove anything with this single parenthood! They are endangering the lives of their children."

That night, as Thapelo visited, Bola thought it would be nice to have a conversation with him. "Could you tell me a bit about your family?" he asked. "Your dad and your mom and everyone?"

Thapelo felt choked. "I never met my dad. I literally only heard about him. My mom is in Durban. She is a sit-at-home mom. I have two elder brothers. I don't know where they are."

Bola was silent. He could not speak again.

Thapelo was the sink where Bola's semen washed away when he needed to jerk off without stressing himself over women. Bola said women were a tug of war. That to have sex with a woman, one had to sweat and spend a huge amount of time negotiating. For Thapelo, Bola was his unintelligent contact—his source of income. He could tell Bola anything. Since he met Bola, he had never looked for another way to feed himself. Bola gave him money to buy his iPhone, paid for his tuition and sent him money via e-wallet in the middle of the night, to settle any bill. He was not going to lose his ATM to any stupid woman in Nigeria. It was either Bola stayed with him, or he would blackmail him with the information he was keeping on him.

"What are we, Bola?" Thapelo asked Bola, as he lay on the couch, watching a film on Netflix.

Bola turned to him. "What are we?"

"Yes."

Bola laughed. "You are funny," he said. "Do you expect me to marry a man? For what reason would I marry a man?"

"Then, you are literally deceiving me." Bola had told him in the past that any man who loved a man because of money and iPhones was a hypocrite. "If the man willingly gives the money," Thapelo tried to defend his foolishness, "he loves the man."

"You are deceiving yourself," Bola said. "Not me. You like money and phones. You now want marriage, so I can keep buying all these things for you."

Thapelo never expected Bola to punch him from the angle that he did. He remained calm.

"Do you know what I find funny about you South Africans?" Bola asked.

Thapelo shook his head.

"You love money, but you don't know how to get it," Bola said. "You love booze, but you don't know how to keep the supplies coming. So, when you find your kwerekwere that has money, you want to do anything to keep them, so they can keep spending for you."

Thapelo walked into the bedroom and shut the door loudly.

"And you South Africans hate hearing the truth."

Bola had been prepared for that night. He knew it would come. He was ready. People had told him, that one day, Thapelo would take advantage of his vulnerability, but he was never going to let that happen.

All these memories came rushing back to Thapelo, as he sat with Chamai in the bar of The Bannisters Hotel. Thapelo was lodging in room 57. He had been there for two days now and knew Bola was at Protea Hotel, close to De Bliss Pub and Grub, which was owned by a Nigerian and served Nigerian cuisines like oha, egusi, ogbono, onugbu, ugu and uziza soups, with eba and pounded yam. He pretended as if he wanted to eat there, so he could keep looking for Bola. He discovered—from whoever his source was—that Bola was in the hotel with his fiancé. He spent some time in the hotel lobby, waiting, and when he could not see Bola, he disappeared to search all the hangouts and bars that Nigerians frequented in Braamfontein.

But Bola had seen him already. He knew what the idiot was up to and asked Chike to help him. Chike and Bola had known each other for a while since they came to South Africa. Bola would tell Chike in Pidgin, "For dis Southy, you go hustle for Joburg, go spend de dough for Cape Town."

When they spoke on the phone, Chike had asked Bola to meet him at The Spurs on Jorissen Street. It was a close to The Bannister's and he knew it was where Thapelo was staying. Someone had warned Thapelo that Nigerians were more united outside

Nigeria, that they were a mafia united against the enemy and that if he tried anything stupid, the Nigerians would gang up and take him out but Thapelo's hatred and anger and vindictive spirit led him on.

Chike was talking to Bola now. "You no suppose allow dis ting reach dis level." He kept talking, as they sat opposite each other. "Homosexuals dey vindictive. Dem dey like out everyone. Dem dey like tell everyone say everyone na homo. That boy is ready to even come into the room where you are with your fiancé and tell her."

"So, wetin I go do?" Bola was confused.

"I go send person wey go kpai the boy," Chike assured him he would send someone to kill Thapelo. "Homosexuals are vindictive." He repeated. "If they want to out you, they will. Best to kill this one, before your fiancé finds out."

They both stood up to leave.

Bola said, "I appreciate you, my brother."

"You're welcome," Chike said. "Don't joke with these people. They are after money. Do not let him have it. You will hear from me when it is done."

Chamai rubbed his palms around a bottle of Corona inside the restaurant of The Bannisters. He was waiting for Thapelo, who waltzed in with his bum shorts and rucksack. When Thapelo received the call from Chamai, he did not ask many questions.

"So," Thapelo said, as he sat opposite Chamai and ordered a gin and tonic, "You said you are from Zim?"

"Yes," Chamai said, sipping from his bottle.

In the background, Oliver Mtukudzi's Mutserendende played.

"What a coincidence!" Thapelo said and gesticulated. "We were literally talking about Zim, and Oliver's voice literally appeared!"

Thapelo suddenly became animate because of how handsome Chamai was. Chamai was the kind of man Thapelo wanted.

After they finished their drinks, Chamai and Thapelo walked to the reception. Thapelo told Chamai his room number and asked him to walk upstairs and wait for him, so he could get his key. Chamai walked the staircase, slowly, taking his time, because the elevator was not working. As he climbed, he counted the steps. He counted how long this mission would take. The sound of Chike's voice was in his head. Chike had called him up and asked him to do this. Chike had made him a huge offer. He needed the money. He needed the money. He needed the money he kept reassuring himself.

When Chike had called Chamai, he had said, "You go do this work very clean."

"Mzansi people think say Naija people no get sense," Chike continued.

Chamai nodded.

Chike spoke angrily. He said South Africans thought Nigerians were not smart. "Do you know why?"

"No."

"You don't know?"

"No."

"Let's find out from our friend, Thapelo," Chike said sarcastically. "Ask him why he thinks he could make a Nigerian his target. I tell these young South Africans to go and work hard for money. They think they can make money through blackmail and begging for an e-wallet.

The room was dark when Thapelo and Chamai entered. As Thapelo turned on the switch by the door, a bright light flooded the space, showing the small bed on the right. There was a small TV, too, mounted to the wall. The bath was on the left. Chamai began to think of the vigorous scuffle he would have to accomplish his mission. He was not sure he would succeed today. His heart raced.

Thapelo looked at him sensually. "What do you want to do, hey?" he asked.

Chamai was not sure what he meant. Then it struck him. He was not challenging him to do what he initially came to do. He wanted to know what he wanted sexually.

"Whatever you offer me," Chamai said and smiled.

"Let's do it, hey!"

Thapelo slowly undressed. He dropped his rucksack to the floor. He removed his shoes before removing his bum short. He removed his shirt. As he did this, so did Chamai, whose clothes came off quickly. Chamai stood in his white briefs.

"Ever tried it in a bathtub?" Chamai asked Thapelo.

He shook his head. "I would like to, hey," Thapelo added. "It is literally my dream."

They slowly moved to the bathtub and Chamai let the water run. He took the remote control of the TV and increased the volume. It was PSquare singing.

"I love Nigerian music," Chamai said.

"Me, too," Thapelo said.

The music blasted. Chamai hugged Thapelo and, by now, the water had filled up the tub. Chamai moved and held Thapelo tightly by his neck, pretending to kiss him. Thapelo felt utterly relaxed. He threw his head back, and Chamai held it strongly under the water. As Thapelo tried to scream, Chamai pinned him down. He began to thrash. The music played on. The more Thapelo tried to free himself, the more he realised he could not hear the music. Chamai held him right there, his legs dangling in the air. Thapelo struggled and struggled until his legs went still. Chamai held him until he stopped breathing. He checked his pulse, before squeezing his neck once more.

Chamai removed his hands from his neck and slowly stepped out of the bathtub.

10

PLOTTING THE JOB

Papi leans back in his seat, briefcase on the desk. He is listening to Chike, who stands before him reporting that nothing has happened since he travelled to Cape Town. Everywhere is calm and business is steady, he tells Papi.

"You see Ruth since I travel?" Papi asks.

"I go her apartment go help her run something yesterday."

"Wetin be that?"

"Her fridge spoil. I help her fix am."

"I see," Papi says. "Talking about that, she give you my money?"

Chike produces a large envelope thick with money from his waist. "Everything dey inside here. Plus, wetin I collect from all the boys."

Taking the envelope, Papi pulls out the cash and

places it on his desk. "Come," he motions to Chike, "sidon, make we balance this money".

Chike settles himself into the chair opposite Papi, who in turn, takes out a large calculator from his desk drawer. Just then, the buzzer to the corridor's security gate goes off. Papi sees Osas looking up at him in the monitor. He lets him through and watches him stroll down the corridor. When he gets to the office door, he pushes the second buzzer and lets him through.

Osas strides into the room, happy to see Chike there. He will enjoy this. "My boy got information he wan sell to you Papi," he says, smiling down at Chike.

Chike snorts, "Wetin you have boy?"

"Shut up!" Papi admonishes Chike. "And?" he sits back in his chair, looking expectantly at Osas.

"The Francophones go move on Buccaneers with large haul of baking soda," Osas says proudly.

"True?" asks Papi.

"True, my boy dey speak French. Him hear everything for Francophone bar," Osas beams handing Papi this information. Chike is visibly upset.

"You go gather all the boys come, Chike. Osas get big job wey dey ground. I wan make we start to plan am."

Chike stands, glares at Osas, then leaves.

"Come, sidon. Tell Papi everyting."

Chike has just walked into the darkened private room at the back of the barbershop where he finds half a dozen Nigerian men working, undistracted, on an array of open laptops. The glow of the laptop screens are the only faint light in the room. Kayode is busy inspecting what the crew is doing, giving directions and patting his colleagues on the back.

"Na the work we dey do today be that," Kayode says. "Ali portal just open and we get credit cards wey go expire by midnight. So na to shop be our work today."

"Since when be this?" Chike asks.

"We dey here since yesterday." Kayode goes over to a table with a laptop. He takes a showman's swig from an open bottle of Johnnie Walker. "Man gats work," he smiles, wiping his mouth.

"Una don sleep at all?"

"Wetin be sleep when hustle dey?" Kayode replies.

Chike chuckles and finds himself a seat. Images on the TV catch his attention. A news report shows a covered body on a gurney being rolled out of a building in an industrial area. A couple of police officers stand around looking serious. Curious, Chike picks up the remote and increases the volume. A passport image of the client that Chike had arranged for Chamai appears on the TV.

A female reporter is saying, "After the owner of the hotel found the corpse of a foreigner. An autopsy is yet to be performed, but injuries on the neck suggest that the man, wanted by Interpol concerning human trafficking, had his throat torn out. Police are asking that anyone with any information should please come forward urgently. We'll come back with more as soon as there are fresh developments".

Chike is in a daze. The news has made both his mind and pulse race. This could lead back to him, he realises. He had supplied both the drugs and Chamai to the man who had paid him well above the usual rates. He had pocketed the excess without Don Papi knowing anything. Murdered? Chamai? The scene at the coffee shop plays out once more in Chike's mind. This explained Chamai's strange behaviour at the coffee shop.

"Wetin happen?" Kayode asks, snapping him out of his reverie. "Na your brother?"

"Idiot!" Chike hisses. "My brother dey Naija dey fuck your mama."

"Which mama? The one wey don die since abi?"

Chike does not laugh. He is not in the mood. He gets up. "See, e get matter wey carry me come. E be like big operation dey ground. Boss say make you show him office this night."

"What time?"Kayode asks, equally serious now.

Chike is already heading out. "Eight o'clock."

Striding down the street, Chike takes out his phone and dials. There is a series of buzzes but no connection. He smiles nonetheless then types a message and clicks the Send button.

Chamai is lying on his mattress on the floor, staring at the ceiling, when his phone rings. Seeing Chike's name flashing on the screen, he silences the call. Seconds later, a text comes through. He ignores it for a while before reading.

The message is in bold: I KNOW YOU KILLED THAT GUY. PICK UP THE PHONE IF YOU DON'T WANT ME TO HEAD TO THE COPS WITH THIS.

His heart stops. He has enough money to leave, to try to disappear, but he knows the Nigerians have connections everywhere and being chased by both the police and them is something he cannot foresee himself doing.

His phone rings again, interrupting his thoughts.

He hesitates to pick up but does. "I told you to leave me alone."

"Even the cops no want leave you alone," Chike says, unmistakable joviality in his voice. "Where you dey?"

"I'm not at home."

"Wherever you be, meet me the usual place this afternoon. We need to talk."

Osas is bent over, tying his shoelaces in the modestly furnished spare bedroom of Andre's apartment.

"Out early today?" Andre, who has just woken up, asks.

"Yes."

Andre crosses to the kitchen.

Osas stands and buckles his belt before heading for the front door.

"Osas!"

Osas stops and then hurries through to the kitchen. Andre, in boxer shorts and a sleeveless shirt that shows off his rippling muscles, is in front of the open refrigerator, a carton of milk in hand.

"Wetin happen?" Osas asks.

"The milk is gone. And I didn't drink it." Throwing the carton into the bin, he picks up a twelve-tray egg carton on the table and shakes it in Osas' face. "The eggs are gone too. And I didn't finish that either." He throws up his arms in exasperation. "Come on, man!"

"Sorry," Osas says. "I'll buy on my way back."

"You shouldn't be. Those girls you bring here should be the sorry ones."

"Sorry."

"Fucking stop apologising!"

Osas nods. Andre being grumpy when he wakes is something Osas has had to get used to. "See you later."

Shortly after Osas leaves, Andre puts on his shoes to go out for breakfast. He walks along the alley to a McDonald's, whistling, when Kunta in a leather jacket and the huge Omoro step out of a doorway and block his way.

"What's this for?" he demands, nerves immediately prickling, not knowing whether they knew about the information Osas had helped him sell.

"Ever since yoosee us we bin watchin yoo, boy," Kunta says. "And we no you are wit de Nigewians."

"Fuck no!" Andre tries to deny.

"Shut up!" Omoro snarls.

"Yoo even got one of dem living wit yoo," Kunta

continues. "Now listen. Don come sniffin round us no more. Keep a yor tail out of de Nigewian dealings cos you don know der half of it. And wemember, if we wan pay yoo a visit, we know where find yoo. Now scwam, wabbit." He shoves Andre hard against the wall, before marching off down the alleyway.

"So, you been want make I first threaten you before you come?"

They are seated at an isolated table in the Our Blend coffee shop.

"I've told you, I don't want to do it anymore," Chamai replies.

"But you no get choice."

"What if I say I do?"

Chike smiles. He passes a piece of paper across the table to Chamai. "The address is written there. The appointment na this night. Eleven o'clock."

Chamai glares at him with beastly intensity.

"And if you never dey there by eight-thirty," Chike goes on casually, "then you better be far from Braamfontein, cos I gon call de cops and we gon come for you too."

Fear creeps into Chamai's eyes. He knows what they are capable of. What will happen to him in prison, his only other option? "You're blackmailing me. You know this is shit, right?"

"This world a shitty place, Chamai."

Snatching the paper, Chamai hurries out without another word.

Chike smiles and reclines on his seat. He had a boy no more; he now had a prey. This was going to be fun.

At midnight, Papi's office is crowded. There is Osas, Chike, Kayode, and Maskotoe – all of the Nigerian syndicate. The big man sits behind his desk, a sombre expression on his face. Everyone's phone is on the table, their batteries are taken out.

"The operation wey dey ground na big one," Papi says, his tone deathly, a ruthless general about to embark on a definitive mission.

Some kilometres away from Papi's office, members of the Francophone gang are gathered in their closed bar. Kunta stands in their midst, addressing them, his eyes darting and murderous. He speaks clearly to them all: "It involves a vehicle full of high-end jewelwy and coca..."

Papi is saying, "Just one car, no security escort vehicle, and na for night them dey enter Braamfontein. When Francophones hit, we hit the Francophones."

The gang hangs on every word Kunta is saying, "We need disable de dwiver and one security detail in fwont and we got der loot."

"But won't de got guns?" someone asks.

"Sure them go don finish the packin," Papi says. "Na where you come in be that, Maskotoe."

They all turn in Maskotoe's direction.

"I got the guns," Maskotoe smiles.

"Asides fwom pistols, we need at least two AK47 wifles and a smoke gwenade. Quick and easy. Not too many guys," Kunta says.

"Twee enough?" Omoro asks.

Papi assures them. "Five men go do the job. Osas go

dey lookout. Him go need walkie-talkie, Chike note."

Chike nods all attention.

"Three others for the surprise, I drive."

⚜

"We should be in out thirty minutes tops," Kunta replies. "Any oder question?"

⚜

Kayode has a question. "Who go dey in charge of the getaway car?"

"Na you go steal car tonight," Papi answers. "We meet again tomorrow to review."

⚜

The Francophone gang finished with the operation arrangements.

"We about be millionaires," Kunta promises.

⚜

Papi has a grin on his lips. "By the time we done, everybody here go collect better bar." They have no idea what is coming.

Part 3

CONFIRMATION

Where there is no struggle, there is no strength.
— Oprah Winfrey

THE HORROR

There are red roses in elaborate vases and lit candles in silver stick holders scattered around the rented apartment. A romantic gesture. Sprawled out on his stomach on the large bed, a grey-haired, goateed pink man in his late forties daydreams while he waits for the black boy to come out of the shower. He is thinking about his last tryst in this room that he uses only for occasions like this. He had thrust into that boy until his excitement had built to unimaginable heights. When he had hit his climax, his thighs had quaked feverishly.

He is hoping for that again, to moan uncontrollably once more. He had never had it that good before. There is just something about black boys that is irresistible to him –beautiful and inexplicable. He closes his eyes, letting all the dazzling feelings a faux marriage has deprived him. Margaret would never understand even if he had enough courage to tell her that while he cared for her, he never loved her. Perhaps someday, he would be man enough to tell her that their two-decade marriage had no future; that he had always preferred being with men. What would she call him? A faggot? Would she scream and hit his chest? Or would she do nothing, maybe do him a favour and just sign the divorce papers as quickly as possible. He needed to think this through. In the meantime, he would not stop booking appointments with these male prostitutes that let him fuck the devil out of them.

He hears the shower stop and the bathroom door open and turns over lazily to have a glimpse of the naked boy. He does not manage to see much, for a pillow presses down his face with such fierceness that it suffocates him. He thrashes about, clawing for dear life. *What is going on?* He wants to scream but his voice comes out muffled. Reaching for the assailant's wrists, he tries to wrestle them away, but he is not as strong as the other person is. *Was this death?* Just when he thinks the pressure is relaxing, something hard is brought down viciously upon his head. The world explodes into a light, and his head begins a wild spin. Repeatedly, the blow comes down, until his numbness becomes absolute.

Blood stains the sheets and pillows. Some has dropped onto the tiled floor. Chamai sits naked on the bed, a bloodied candlestick holder in his hand. He is crying. This is not what he came to this country for, he thinks. He had fled from the disaster of his village, and here he was, trapped in this horror of his own making.

Osas' hand is on April's waist as he knocks on the door. She has a shopping bag in her right hand. The door opens a fraction. It is Andre answers the door, but the door chain stays on.

"How far guy? Open door na," Osas says.

"No, Oscar," Andre answers, glancing at April. "Besides, you never listen."

"Haba guy! Na just this night, she go leave first thing in the morning."

Andre shakes his head. "No, she can't stay. And neither can you."

Osas stares at him.

"You've got to go, Osas."

"We no fit discuss am?" he asks. He takes the parcel from April and lifts it. "See, I don buy eggs and milk."

"Keep it, I'm sure you'll need it," Andre says. "I'll grab your bag."

Outside Andre's apartment building, Osas drops his travelling bag on the floor wearily.

"So, wetin we go do now?" April asks.

"Go back una hotel; I go find where I go sleep." He fetches for his wallet and singles out some money. "Na only taxi you fit see this kind time."

April pushes the money back at him. "No worry, I carry small money. Na your own matter concern me. Where you can enter now?"

Osas returns the money to his pocket and flags down a passing taxi. The minibus halts and April climbs inside.

"I go call you tomorrow," she says.

Osas nods and watches the vehicle get swallowed by traffic and distance.

When Ruth opens the door after the second knock, she is startled to see Osas standing before the door, a large travelling bag slung over his shoulder. She takes a perfunctory glance back inside the apartment and then leans closer.

"Wetin you dey do for here?" she hisses, barely above a whisper.

Osas was not expecting this welcome. "I need a place to sleep."

"Keep your voice down!"

"Ruth, na who dey there?" a voice calls out from the apartment. There is no mistaking its Papi.

Osas' jaw drops.

"Na my neighbour o," Ruth calls back over her shoulder. She makes an "*I'll-call-you*" sign with her hand, waves him away and shuts the door.

Osas hurries off, feeling the weight of isolation and abandonment crashing down. The memory of Oghogho running away into the crowd comes flashing through his mind again. He does not have the strength to steel himself against the wave of emotions surging through him.

Alone, Chike settles down on the couch, cradling a bowl of cereal. He turns on the television and flicks through the news channels. Images splash onto the screen. A body draped over with a sheet is being rolled away on a gurney onto a waiting ambulance.

A reporter gestures at the body as she speaks into a microphone. Chike almost drops his bowl, trying to turn the volume up:

> *"A body has been found in what is looking to be a sex motivated serial murder case. housekeeper at an apartment at 1156 Golan Heights* discovered the body. *At this time, the police are interviewing the neighbours and have said they will issue an official statement soon. The police have asked anyone with information to come forward urgently. We will come back to you as more insight unfolds on this breaking story. Atandwa Lembede, BBN News."*

Chike stares at the screen. A smile takes shape on his face: a smile that anyone would be a fool to trust.

12

BRAAMFONTEIN BLUES

Detectives Booysen, Jiba, and Radebe of the Special Operations Directorate are at their desks in the sparsely furnished room when Booysen's phone rings. He picks up. "Ja, hello." He listens for a bit and then hangs up.

"What's new?" asks Jiba.

"They found the boy. We know where to pick him up. Let's go," Booysen says, standing.

Detective Jiba snatches his badge and gun from his desk drawer.

Osas watches silently as Papi counts the bundle of cash. Just as the big man finishes with the last stack, the buzzer for the outside gate sounds. The intrusion irritates Papi. One glance at the monitor and his face contorts.

"Police," he says.

Osas is unsure of what to do, but Papi lets the police in. He watches with surprising calm as they stride down the corridor. Shoving the money into the bottom drawer of his desk and locking it, he sits back and looks at Osas. "You carry exhibit for your body?"

Osas shakes his head. "No, boss, nothing."

"Open up," a voice shouts through the door.

Papi buzzes the police into his office and then places his hands lazily behind his head.

Half a dozen police officers led by Detective Jiba and Booysen pour inside, guns at the ready.

"You cannot search here without a warrant," Papi states, calmly.

"We're not here for you," Detective Booysen replies. He points at Osas as two police officers move to cuff him. "We want him."

Osas is shocked.

"We're taking you in for questioning," Detective Jiba says.

"What he does?" Papi asks, and then shouts at Osas. "Wetin you do!"

"Your questions will be answered if you come to the station," Officer Booysen replies. He says to

Osas. "Anything you say from this point on can and will be used against you in the courts. Let's go."

Osas is entirely perplexed as the officers force his hands behind his back and snap the cold handcuffs on his wrists.

"No tell them anything," Papi instructs Osas. "I dey come later."

The police officers guide Osas out of the room.

The fact that he was in the same bare interrogation room as last time makes Osas nervous. The same officer, Booysen, now stares at him in silence. Osas wondered if this had something to do with the Francophone gang incident. The last time he was here, he had been the victim. Now he was being treated differently.

"We have good cause to suspect you, Omorogie," Detective Booysen says, "of murder."

"What?" Osas shakes his head. Unbelievable! He had not committed any murder.

"Where were you on the night of the twenty-sixth of July?"

Osas was not going to let these men keep him here any longer than they already had for something he had had not done. He remembered that night.

"My roommate pursue me comot for house. I been dey look for where I go sleep. Because una see me no mean say na me do am." Then he added hastily, "I been go visit my friend".

"And what's your friend's address?"

"Apartments de Medicis"

The two detectives exchange glances. "The Italian Expatriate quarters?"

"Yes."

"What's your friend's name?"

"Ruth."

"And where can we find her?"

Osas stares at them. Was it a smart thing to rope Ruth into this mess?

"Where can we find this friend of yours?" Detective Jiba repeats.

Osas swallows hard.

"Apartment 447."

Ruth is now in an interrogation room of her own. Detectives hurl questions her way.

"Do you affirm that the young man who goes by the name of Osas visited you on the night of the twenty-sixth of July?"

"Yes," Ruth says.

"Yes, what?" Detective Booysen asks aggressively. He knows who this woman is, but it is better to act as if he does not.

"Yes. Him been dey with me."

"How long did he spend in your apartment? Can you remember the exact times?"

"I no fit remember exact time but him been stay for long time, maybe from six pm to ten or eleven pm. I no dey sure."

"What is your relationship with him and what was he doing there during that time?"

"Osas na my boyfriend boy," she tells them. "Him dey work for my boyfriend and he come help me to fix shelf for my kitchen."

Detective Booysen is thoughtful and silent for a time. "I have no further questions for you right now, but if we need you, we'll let you know."

Papi strides into the police station in the company of a pink attorney wearing an expensive suit. He halts on the steps on seeing Osas and Ruth walking along the hallway, flanked by Detectives Jiba and Booysen.

Ruth is visibly surprised to run into Papi here. Osas lowers his head to the floor.

"Wetin you dey do for here?" she asks.

"Na wetin I go ask you be that," Papi says, frowning. "No be for my office them arrest Osas?"

The lawyer steps up to the officers confidently. "I'm to represent the young man."

"That is not necessary anymore as they have been let go," Detective Booysen explains. "He was brought in for questioning concerning a murder that took place on the 26th of July. But since the lady corroborates his whereabouts, and the security footage from the building clearly shows him entering and leaving at the time of interest, the young man has been let go."

Papi looks at Ruth to see that her face could not be more relaxed. "So de matter don finish?" he turns to the detectives.

"At this time, yes."

A furious Papi barges into his office, followed timidly by Osas. The big man takes a seat behind his desk, hands shaking. "Osas," he pauses for a long time, "wetin you go do for Ruth house?"

"Boss, I no been dey her house," he begins.

"Why you come tell them say na there you been dey?"

"I been go sell market for person inside the building that night. And I no fit tell them say na market I go sell for there."

"So, how you take know say na there Ruth dey stay?"

"I don dey go sell market there before, boss. I don see Madam Ruth for the compound before."

Papi grinds his teeth. "Osas, make you dey very careful. You dey hear me so?"

Osas nodded. "Yes boss. I hear you."

Papi tells him he can go. But Papi did not get to his present position by being a fool.

⟡

In the past.

Morning arrives over Braamfontein with obvious reluctance. It is cold, surprisingly so. The previous night had been worse, and the chill had only abated somewhat with the sluggish approach of day. A garbage truck makes the rounds. It seems to be the only thing alive at that hour, bearing witness to the stillness of a cold silvery dawn.

Chike digs his hands into the pockets of his woollen jacket and stamps his feet to fight off the cold. He longs for the warmth of his room and his duvet, but he has to be out of bed at the agreed time. It would be bad to keep his boss waiting. Better to arrive early and wait for Papi.

From his vantage point at a street corner, Chike scans the vicinity. It is calm and lonely all around as far as he can see. The weather appears to have lulled Braamfontein to sleep. These parts are safe, a territory under the loose control of three weak Nigerian cartels that all get along well with each other. Still, his basic survival instincts will never let him feel at ease.

Hurried footsteps approach from the distance. He looks in its direction to see a girl. Her strides are brisk, and she hugs her coat closely about her. Her bare legs are exposed. A prostitute, definitely. Her job for the night is done, and she must be hurrying along to her madam or to wherever her abode may be. Perhaps she works independently.

She rounds the corner and suddenly sees Chike. She is startled. Instinctively her hand flies to her handbag. Chike smiles at her and holds up his hands in mock surrender. Relieved he poses no danger, she hurries along, quickening her strides. Chike watches her. He can tell her calves are strained with the effort of walking fast. He wonders why women wear high heels even though they do not seem comfortable in them. What if she needs to run, he wonders.

A car approaches. There is no mistaking Papi's Mercedes. It breaks in front of him. He gets into the front passenger seat. Papi drives off almost immediately.

"Good morning, boss."

Papi grunts a reply. Chike steals a look at the big man. His face is set on the road in front of them. He drives quite fast. The steering wheel seems too small in his powerful hands, as though he can easily rip it off the dashboard. A gold ring glints on the middle finger of his right hand. There is no telling what is on the big man's mind and would be futile to guess. His strained look gives nothing away. There is hardly a time when his countenance looks any different. Chike will have to wait until Papi speaks. Until then, he will have to keep mum.

For a fleeting moment, Chike toys with the idea of reaching for the car stereo. Some music would be good to cut the tension. He gives up the idea; he is not on such a familiar ground with Papi. It is better not to do anything that his boss would consider overreaching and disrespectful. Such a mistake could cause him a fall from grace, or much worse.

They hit a highway, cruising along at over a hundred and twenty on the speedometer. Gone are the city sights and cluttered residential buildings. Instead, there are vast stretches of untouched land occasionally dotted by telltale signs of some ongoing government or corporate project. A good hour stands between them and their destination. Chike settles into looking out of the window. He does not realise when his eyelids begin to get heavy and droop over.

They arrive fifteen minutes earlier than Chike had expected. Papi guides the Mercedes into the lone parking lot. He gets out and secures the automated lock after Chike and together, they walk up the block to a metal door built into a brick building. Papi pounds at the door with the base of his fist. While they wait for the door to be answered, Chike scans the vicinity, his hand tucked into his jacket.

Papi looks assured.

There is no hint of apprehension about him, even though Chike could swear the big man's demeanour is all but deceiving; there is simply no way the man would venture out of his territory unloaded.

A bolt clangs and the door opens. A lanky young man holds it open, blocking the entrance. From his hair and the geometry of his face, there is no mistaking his Ethiopian descent.

"I want see your boss," Papi says to the Ethiopian.

"One minute," the young lad says and shuts the door in their faces. Presently, he returns and ushers them in. A small hallway opens into a sizeable indoor space. From the pole on the lighted stage and the arrangements about the place, Chike can tell it is a strip club. It is closed at this time of the day. A burly African mops the floors at the farthest end. A heavily tattooed bartender looks up from cleaning his work area. He nods at Chike who meets his eyes.

"Please come this way," the Ethiopian says to Papi. He leads Papi and Chike further away from the room to a door. He knocks and turns the handle without waiting for an invitation. Papi breezes into the office like some Roman Emperor's envoy coming to see a governor of one of the provinces. Chike trails behind ever watchful with his hands to his sides. There is no need to create wrong impressions.

A slender man in an ill-fitting leather jacket sits behind a gleaming desk. Without a doubt, he is Ethiopian too, and a dandy at that. His prominent gold necklace, wristwatch and bejewelled fingers say as much. There is a line of cocaine laid out on the table.

"Welcome, welcome," he says, getting up to shake their hands, then returns to his desk. He Snorts out the line of cocaine with a rolled-up currency note and leans back into his seat with his eyes shut. For a few moments, nothing seems to matter to him until he comes to. "Please sit down," he says, gesturing at the seats across from him.

Papi and Chike settle in.

"Nice to see you in these parts again. I hope your trip wasn't eventful?"

"No problems at all, Omar. I come for business, so distance no matter."

"Nigerians," Omar says to himself, chuckling with pleasure. "I like you guys."

"So make we talk business. You know time is money."

"I could get you something to drink."

"No worry. We dey okay like this."

"Okay," Omar says resignedly.

"I want your girls to deliver some consignment for me for Brazil."

Omar sits up. "You mean, coke?"

"Yes. Coke. And I want only South African girls."

Omar seems to ponder something over. "That could come with its own challenge. You know how the South African ones are."

"Those ones na sure bet. With them, we no go get problems for airports, especially for the South African side."

"Okay, I see. What's in it for me?"

"Twenty per cent. And you make sure you give us correct babes."

"Thirty per cent is what I have in mind. I will be running this along with my partner. You know him, right?"

"Yes, I know Lethabo. But thirty per cent too high."

"No. It's a fair rate."

"You know how things dey go. This na our first time. Make we do business."

"Papi, you know you're a good businessman and I have deep respects for you. I will want to do business with you anytime."

"Oya, make we leave am for twenty-five. I believe say twenty-five good for everybody."

"Fair enough."

They both shake hands in agreement.

"I'll put things together with Lethabo right away and I will call you to receive the girls."

"I go dey wait for your call."

Papi gets up. He shakes hand with Omar again and leaves the office with Chike close behind. The bartender in the club has vanished and the burly African has progressed to another section of the bar. There is a girl on a stool now, smoking. She looks Indian. Obviously, one of the strippers. One look at her and you can tell how pissed she is. The lanky Ethiopian sees them to the door.

Papi says nothing as he drives back to Braamfontein. Chike guesses Papi's mind is on the money and the possibility of making more if Omar's girls successfully make three runs. Things would have looked much better if he were to use Ruth's girls, but they are all Nigerian. It would have greatly reduced the expected cost of operation. The Nigerian passport in itself attracts too much attention to the bearer at every foreign port of entry. He has to play it safe. Hence the South Africans.

RED ALL OVER

Chike likes that the afternoon is mild. It is going to drizzle. He nods to the jazz music playing from a loudspeaker at the Our Blend, as he sips from a steaming cup of tea. Chamai walks through the door, spots him, and joins him at the table.

"What now?" Chamai demands.

Chike simply pulls a piece of paper out of his breast pocket and hands it to Chamai. "Him name na Steve. Na him get the only massage parlour for that plaza."

Chamai laughs in Chike's face. "So, I'm supposed to go fuck him in there or what?"

"You no dey fuck this one."

Chamai stares coldly at him, not quite understanding. His eyes narrow when Chike unzips his jacket, takes out a piece of folded paper, unfolds it, and spreads it out on the table for Chamai to see. A stick man, in a childish colour drawing, has bludgeoned another with what looks to be a hammer. The red colour is splashed all over the page. Chamai looks at Chike, aghast.

"You're going to kill him," Chike says flatly, a cruel smile on his lips.

"No," says Chamai, the horror obvious in his eyes.

"You can and you will. You don kill two already. You wan go jail for them and become lady boy?"

Chamai stares hard at Chike. His hatred for this Nigerian has reached its limit.

"If I were you, I'd go fix the target now," Chike laughs, taking another sip of his tea and looking around in a gesture to Chamai that the conversation is finished.

The moment Chamai leaves the coffee shop, Chike's phone rings. He swipes at the screen. "KY, how far?"

"Chykoe! I just receive Intel now for Facebook. Killer Priest don mud," Kayode announces excitedly from the other end.

Chike sits upright. "Wetin happen?"

"Buccaneers and Axe men don start war for Naija since yesterday."

"Wetin be scores?"

"Na 2-2 I hear."

"Mehn. We gats dey careful for this side. You know say those boys blood dey hot."

"Taah! Them no born them well!" Kayode says.

His confidence makes Chike smile.

"Anyway, I don tell you my own. Just dey careful. I dey come."

Steve is lounging in the empty massage parlour when the bell rings. He stands to open the gate, as it is still too early for the manager's shift. A skinny looking black boy in denim jeans and a Nike T-shirt stands at the gate.

"Yes?" Steve inquires. "We aren't open yet."

"Hi, that's okay," Chamai, offers. "I'd like to make a booking with you for tonight. It is my birthday. I'm twenty-one," Chamai adds.

"OK, sure. Come inside," Steve presses the buzzer for the security gate and then leads Chamai to the reception desk. "So, what can we offer you? There's a full-body, neck rub, foot—"

"I'm looking for something a bit different," the boy interrupts Steve. "Something extra, aside from the massage."

Steve chuckles. He is used to young men trying to use the right language. "Oh, like a happy ending you mean?"

"Yeah, something like that."

"I'm sorry I didn't get your name?"

"Everybody calls me Harry," Chamai says.

Steve's smile grows broader at the boy's lack of experience. "OK. I can see you are not from around here. Is this your first time?"

Chamai looks away. "Yes".

"And tell me, Harry." There is a pause. "Would you like a girl? Or a boy?"

Chamai hesitates for a moment before answering. "A boy, please."

Steve contemplates Chamai for a moment. "Let me make a call." He reaches for the telephone on the desk, but at the exact time that he lifts the receiver to his ear, a hammer smashes against his temple. Steve crumples heavily to the floor. Chamai instinctively knows that the man is dead, just as dead, he realises, as he feels.

14

THE WEB OF KARMA

Osas and Ruth lay under the sheet of the bed, both naked and exhausted from their lovemaking.

"Bad boy! Small pikin like you, see wetin you sabi do."

Osas is flattered. "Small pikin ke? Man wey don clock nineteen years, na still small boy?"

"You be lion, no be lie."

His ego swells like cooking rice. "Na wetin my grandmama been dey call me. The lion."

"Your mama nkor?" Ruth asks.

"I no sabi my mama. She waka comot Nigeria when I still be small pikin."

Ruth is silent. What he has said seems to have struck a nerve. He takes her in his arms. "Shebi, you from …"

"Ekpoma."

Ruth blinks, instantly high-strung and apprehensive.

"Actually, na Benin I grow but Mama Cecilia tell me say na Ekpoma we from," he says in explanation.

She sits up straight in the bed, as though she had been stung. "Mama Cecelia?"

"Yes."

"Na she be your grandmama?"

"Yes. Why your mood change?"

She forces herself to smile. "Noting. E be like say I been sabi your grandmama before I travel."

"You mean am?"

Wordlessly, she climbs out of bed and reaches for the lighter and cigarette that sit on a stool. She drags long and hard, filling her lungs and then lets everything out in a steady stream of smoke. "See eh, Don Papi fit show here anytime. Make you begin dey go."

"Na to pursue me been dey hard you?"

"No be say I dey pursue you. I no want Papi wahala."

Osas hesitantly puts on his clothes and walks to the door, glancing back at Ruth, but she is not looking at him. Her mind is elsewhere. He slams the door on his way out.

Ruth, no longer needing to keep any semblance

of composure, lets the cigarette drop carelessly to the floor. She feels far removed from her present surroundings. "Osanobuwa, wetin I don do?" She covers her face with both her hands. "Wetin I do?"

Osas storms out from Ruth's apartment building, crosses the road, and begins what will be a long and brisk walk through Braamfontein.

From the safety of a newly procured car parked in the distance, Maskotoe, who has been stalking him, picks up his phone. "Boss, him just dey comot from there now."

"You go knack that boy during this operation!" Papi shouts from the other end of the line. "And Maskotoe?"

"Boss?"

"When the time comes, make it hell with my name in his mind."

As Osas walks, he thinks about his life. They say the universe and everything in it is ordered. This could be one of the maybe things in life forever in need of answers. They could still be true. Just maybe. Maybe it was so ordered for Osas, that he would be abandoned

by his mother and left in the care of his grandmother..
Oh, what cruelty. The woman was so bitter with life
and everything about her that everything that met her
bore the stamp of her frustration. And that included
him too. But why? Why did it have to be so? Why
was it so ordered? What was his offence? He wished
someone would tell him. Or was there no longer any
value in all that is being said about cause and effect?
Or did it have to do with his previous life?

They said he is his maternal grandfather
reincarnated, the man to whom his embittered
grandmother was married until he died. He has not
heard anything about the man and has never met
anyone who knew him, but he can bet that the man
was surely not in good terms with his wife. Perhaps
he beat her often or complained so much about her.
Who would not? He would have complained too if
he could get away with it. But he always kept his
complaints inside. No need to bring it to the fore
if he feared repercussions, and grave ones for that
matter.

He had suffered through.

First, it was Chike. One would think the guy is
better off but he is not. He is in a mess as everyone
else —unstable, seeking, searching and finding
nothing but still trudging on and scratching about

for the slightest glimmer of hope or the semblance of it. One could consider his situation worse off in the light of his needs. That which he seeks is elusive, forever out of reach, a cultural anomaly in certain circles and if he is to find it, it will further alienate him, making him all the more solitary and removed from much of the surroundings he had come to know. It happened when he found Senior Odogwu. They became enmeshed in their own world. The world around them became nothing but an outer covering that only existed to protect them and their world. It is just as the covering of a coconut existed with the core but is not a part of it.

However, so much has changed. The world has changed from the days of Senior Odogwu. This was no longer the days of the seminary in Enugu. This is South Africa. He is a grown man and the world had grown alongside him–ever-demanding in its expectations and brutal in its offerings. Alienation would come at a great price and so much would come with it for which he never bargained. Surely, he knows all of this. It must have driven his frustration, and Chamai was no escape for him. He was Chike's alluring nemesis to whom he could never say no.

How does nemesis play out? Does any one of us come into this world for the fulfilment of a particular purpose without being consumed by that same purpose whether or not we fail at it? If Chamai was Chike's nemesis, was he also a victim of nemesis and the order of the universe? Or could it be said that like a floating piece of cork on a lake he simply drifted and drifted until he bumped into Chike, knocking him off the edge and then going the same way? Was everything truly ordered or did it all happen by chance? However much one looked at it, South Africa had been the chessboard where everyone had been assembled like pieces of chess, to be played, one against the other, by whoever called the shots, whoever it was, unseen, omnipresent and decisive. If everyone was played by that hand we call Fate; does it then mean that we should be responsible for the offences that are attributed to us? Or did Fate endue us with passions and desires that run riot so that somehow we could be blackmailed into taking responsibilities for the outcomes of the moves done on the chessboard called Life? Maybe that is what it is. We then may have to exonerate Chike. What about Chamai, drawn from his home like a fluttering night insect hastening away from the nightly darkness, towards the naked flame that is later to consume it and keep it writhing on the ground as it regrets in its final moments for falling for the seduction of the promise of something better?

We will have to exonerate Madam Ruth too. But should we? No, I cannot. That one is everything wrong. What mother would abandon her child and hastily create that much distance between them? What woman would reap from desperation and exploitation of fellow women and still deserve some consideration? But was it exploitation really? Was she not simply seeing demand and taking responsibility for its supply? Maybe we should blame the universe for once; we are all a part of it, it's in every one of us just as it is in Madam Ruth and the much of Braamfontein that constituted a part of her world happened to be her own chessboard, and the girls her pieces. But did she have that much control as a master of the board? Surely not. She is as much a victim like everyone else, a piece in a greater chessboard, playing out her role in the grand scheme of cause and effect and the workings of karma.

Yes, that is what it is. She killed Papi, poisoned him.

He had it coming for him. His entire life had been marked with violence, with him being on the giving end. Maybe we are not to judge him either. He may be but an instrument of the universe, giving and taking as it is ordered. So, who then is to blame him? He is just a victim as everyone else, drawn to South Africa and doing his bit in the grand working of the universe. Then, if he were to reincarnate, what would become of him? Did he live a cause with an effect that is to play out in his next coming? Or was it an effect being played out, of a cause done at some previous time?

In assigning us roles, the universe often apportions to the most important roles to those individuals whom we consider vile. It should be the reason why Satan has so much power and why we approve so much worldly power and influence to vileness. Perhaps such as are vile, in their actions, which cause so many to cringe, are the real custodians of the order of the universe as we feel and know on earth. Maybe if everyone on earth were considered good and easy-going, we would someday, in our goodness evaporate to heaven. Maybe in our goodness, we would fall into a deathly slumber, and the world would become very disorderly as not to suit its fashion as a chessboard for whoever is up there amusing themselves with it.

Papi held the order in Braamfontein. It was upon him that the lives and livelihood of so many were hinged. He protected Ruth's business and her girls and it was he who held in place, the order that attracted everyone else attracted to the chessboard that is Braamfontein – to exercise their activities with karmic consequences even as they played out and affected everyone – including himself, for he is also a chessboard piece after all. Be as it may, he was no pawn. Maybe a knight, but surely not a pawn. He is too important and the fact that he was not given any mean roles further proves this.

Everyone who had been robbed, shot at and, murdered had been part of the universal order. They all had it coming for them by the things they had done or left undone. From the Congolese to the Togolese cartels, Chamai's victims and everyone caught up in the outpouring of greed and deception. Their desires had drawn them out one way or another, to partake of the table laid out for them as the universe had ordered. Then, are they to blame? Perhaps everyone is innocent. We are all victims of the things that keep us unstable and steer us onto the chessboard, to play out our lives as ordered.

Some people seem to be left untouched in this game of life. They bear witness to karma happening to all others. The detectives, Officer Booysen and Officer Julius, seem to number amongst these people. Maybe it is because they are designated very active roles in this game of cause and effect. Maybe the chessboard that is life is of a different kind where chess pieces also keep the rules binding on fellow chess pieces. It could be that they are mere spectators. But who could be a spectator in this life when we have established something as universal as cause and effect? Even the spectators cheer or jeer at some point and these actions could turn out to be causes or effects, as it is.

What about April? What about the pregnancy? Could it be that she, like all others were drawn on to the chessboard that is Braamfontein, to receive or dole out karma? Maybe it is not exactly that same way with her. It could be that she was a balance or karma for Osas. Since he despised whoever sired him for abandoning him, he had played that same hand.

There is this saying that history always repeats itself. It could be happening just like that to Osas. Maybe his father, just like him, had had too much of the weight of life pressing on his shoulders and had to seek an escape out of it all. Everything for him had looked like a web choking the very life out of him. Nothing was incentive enough to stay, not even the baby. He was his father, after all. Maybe he was more of him than the grandfather whom they say reincarnated. Should he be blamed? What if he forgave his father, would that exonerate him from the judgement of others who would be offered insight into the whole situation that he had been a piece in?

15

THE DIVIDED DUO

There are times when Osas wishes he could pass a day without having anything to do with Chike. This afternoon is one of them. Chike's detachment is not sitting well with him. Ever since they left Papi's office that morning, with a parcel and instructions to deliver, Chike has been acting aloof. The guy does not like him. That much is obvious. That dislike for him had made Chike kick him out of his apartment.

There are times when he feels like Chike will feel relieved if he is out of his way. If ever he were to learn about Madam Ruth, Chike would definitely sing the secret to Papi with glee.

"Shebi you carry iron for there?" Chike asks him. It was the third time he spoke to Osas the whole day.

"Yes," Osas replies, tapping his waist to assure him that he had a gun. They walk along the abandoned industrial district and Osas tries to keep up with Chike's hurried strides.

"Where do we go?" Osas asks. "How the area be?"

"Make that one no concern you. Just shine your eyes."

Osas chooses to ignore Chike's attitude. The guy does not see him as a partner. It is too bad, considering that they are supposed to watch each other's backs.

Chike flags down an approaching taxi calls out their destination to the driver and clambers into the back seat. Osas takes the hint and settles into the front next to the South African driver whose head looked newly shaved. He has no facial hair. Bearded South Africans are a very rare sight.

Osas' phone buzzes. It is April. He ignores the call and returns the phone to his pocket. For days, he had been thinking about everything: April, Madam Ruth, himself. It feels like he is getting deeper into a quicksand, with April being attached, and now Madam Ruth's recent irritation. His coming to South Africa had been for a purpose: to make his chances better in life, not to ruin it. He will have to dissociate himself from April. It is the best thing for himself and for her too. None of them will find it easy if ever Madam Ruth were to learn about them.

The phone beeps. It is a text message from April. She says she is not too well, and the test result has come out positive for pregnancy. Impossible! His heart skips. He resists the urge to call her immediately. Instead, he sends her a text, promising to call her later in the day. The shock he feels at the news metamorphoses into anger. Whoever hears of a prostitute getting pregnant like some amateur teen? The whole thing must be intentional. She must be trying to cling onto him.

The taxi pulls over. They arrive at their destination. It is a busy part of town. Chike reaches inside his pocket to pay the driver while Osas gets out, takes a few paces from the taxi and waits. Chike pockets his change and begins to walk without a word or look in Osas' direction. His attitude angers Osas. It is a show of spite. He says nothing as he falls in step with Chike. He no longer knows which makes him more frustrated: Chike's spite or the news of April's pregnancy. What if she is not pregnant? She will have to repeat the test, and this time, he has to be there to see.

They come to a building that looks like a warehouse, but a prominent signpost in front designates it to be a Pentecostal church. Chike walks in. For a moment, Osas hesitates. He thinks about the piece stuck into the waistband of his trousers. The church auditorium is a sizeable one, with rows of plastic white chairs arranged around a central raised carpeted platform on which a glass lectern stands. Artificial flowers adorn strategic parts of the altar, lending the place a hallowed appearance. To one corner of the auditorium, a man in a blue suit is seated with some women. They are obviously having a meeting. Chike makes towards them, followed by Osas. They settle into seats within earshot of the quiet conversation and wait. The man notices them and seems a little perturbed by their presence. Almost immediately, he dismisses the women, and then waves his visitors over.

Osas observes the man up close. He is clean-shaved; his hair is heavily permed, dyed and parted on the side. His mannerisms are exaggerated but there is no missing out his habitual misuse of the 'h' consonant as he speaks.

"Good morning, pastor," Chike greets him.

Osas does the same.

"A good morning to you, too," the man returns, rising to his feet and offering a hand. "I'm Pastor Akande, and you are welcome to Grace Citadel."

"Papi sends us to you,",", Chike says.

Pastor Akande's countenance undergoes a sudden transformation. "Follow me," he says, and leads them to a door at the far corner of the auditorium. It opens into an office. He shuts the door when they are inside, and then he walks over to the desk and sits on its edge without offering Chike and Osas a seat. "How's Papi doing?"

"He's fine," Chike says, handing him an envelope from his pocket.

Pastor Akande accepts the envelope and puts it on the desk next to him.

"He's not acting fine at all," Pastor Akande says, his indigenous accent breaking through his fake mannerisms. "I brought in ten people for him from Nigeria through my crusade. He is not the only one whom I am doing this for. He does not come to pick up as he is supposed to, but what does he do? He delays. I have to hide them in my building. It is very risky. This is the third time he is doing this. The third time!" The pastor runs a hand through his hair. His eyes dart back and forth. "What if information leaks and I get busted by Immigrations? I do not like doing business with illiterates. I am not a tout. I have a reputation and a good standing in the community to protect. And I cannot lose it over some stupidity of some drug dealer who knows nothing about legality and reputation."

"Oga, that matter concern you and Papi. But I no go dey here dey hear you yarn careless about my boss."

"And what will you do?"

Osas can no longer stand Pastor Akande. His insolence is making his mood worse. He gets out his gun.

Pastor Akande scoffs. "That's just what I am talking about. You brought a gun into this premises? So you frighten me with a gun and then what next?"

Osas takes aim and presses the trigger. The bang is loud. Pastor Akande's head looks bloodied at the temple. A small hole lets out a steady stream of blood. Like an effigy, he topples from his perch on the edge of the desk and lands on the floor with a sickening thud.

Chike glances at Osas. There is no telling if his stare is one of disapproval.

"Since I see this man, I no ever like am."

"Me too," Chike says, looking down at the corpse. "No worry, I go explain to Papi. Make we comot here sharp before we cast."

Osas puts his gun away. Chike grabs the parcel off the desk, and they hurry out of the office. There is no one in the church auditorium, and nobody pays them any attention as they step out into the streets and walk away.

Two days later, Osas returns to the police station. He is skeptical but one of the Nigerians at the salon has talked him into going back to the police, this time with a bribe. The encounter with the Congolese guys must have put him under the police radar, the Nigerian had told him, and if he is to ensure things go smoothly for him, it would be best he begins to familiarize himself with the police.

The officer at the counter asks Osas who he wishes to see. He mentions the name of the officer the Nigerian had given him: Officer Kungawo.

"He's not on duty at the moment," the officer tells him. "He'll be available in about three hours."

Osas does not disclose his purpose of visit but promises to check back. He turns down every suggestion that he sees another officer on duty.

The next three hours drag by. Osas passes half the time at a restaurant and the other half window-shopping. Standing outside a jewelry shop, he toys with the idea of getting a beady bracelet for April but shoves the thought away. Two hours and a few minutes pass, and Osas heads back to the police station.

He meets Officer Kungawo, a burly sausage of a man with a jaw that shows signs of drooping any moment. His eyes tell a different story, though. They lend him the disposition of one who belongs to the opposite side of law. They dart here and there, as though naturally disposed to seeking out things concealed.

They are in his office and Osas broaches the matter for which he has come. At first, his reluctance is evident, but Officer Kungawo's directness allays his fears.

"You did well, my friend," he says, accepting the roll of cash, which Osas hands him. He counts the notes, nods his approval and stows the money away in his hip pocket. They exchange phone numbers. "You have nothing to worry for. I got your back."

"Thank you, officer."

"I like good Nigerians. You guys are better than others are. I like doing business with you. As long as you lay low, we'll have no problems and you will be covered in these parts."

"Officer, no worry. I will be paying my dues."

"Good. That's good."

"But officer, I have small problems with the

Congolese people. They are bad for our business."

"You better stay off that lot. Nobody likes them. Not me, either."

"They will execute a hit soon. It is a big job. I have information. Solid one."

Officer Kungawo leans forward, his large hands on the desk. ""My friend, here is my candid advice, and I give it to you as a friend to a friend: stay off the Congolese. Those guys are scared of nothing, not even for their own lives, and surely not of the devil himself. It is a tough job already policing the streets without them, but with them, you don't have any idea about the fears and concerns we have to contend with on a daily basis."

Osas shrugs. "Okay."

"Good," Officer Kungawo says, leaning back in his seat.

Osas gets up to leave. He shakes hands with Officer Kungawo, making to snap his finger in the characteristic Nigerian manner. The gesture turns out awkward, as the South African police officer is unprepared for it.

After Osas has left, Officer Kungawo sits immobile behind his desk. It is looking to be a good day with the promise of many more to come. The bribe money the Nigerian has just given him will go to the installment for his Mercedes. If things continue at this rate, he will be taking the car out of the auto garage sooner than he had expected.

He had taken a liking to the Nigerian instantly, and his name had sounded unique, almost funny. Osas. The guy had brought up something dreadful by ratting on the Congolese and expecting him to get involved. That is one thing with the streets— everyone wants to take out their competition and maintain a monopoly. There is nothing wrong about that, except when it involves the Congolese cartels. No law enforcer in their right mind would ever consider meddling in the business of the Congolese. Especially not when it is being done in the interest and favour of some other cartel. It would be a declaration of war and the Congolese are known to fight dirty. Everyone on the force talks about it, and those tales have struck close to home with two officers he knows personally. A small band of Congolese small-time meth dealers was paying them protection money. The understanding had gone on for many months and things were looking good. The time came when the Congolese guys wanted to step up their game. They set up a meth lab and recruited some more hands, poised to expand their operations. Of course, the officers got a raise to look the other way and give any heads up if their operations got under the radar of the law enforcement agencies. The officers had gotten greedy—the prospects of a promotion on the job were too hard for them to resist. They ratted on the Congolese guys, and the lab was raided. Drugs were seized, most of which went missing months afterwards from the evidence lockers. That was not all. The two police officers had members of their families hacked to death and their tongues cut. The tongues were mailed to the respective officers many months later, freshly preserved and tagged. Even though the officers were promoted, they had been under psychiatric care ever since. As for the Congolese, they had vanished. Every single one of them.

Office Kungawo shudders. Better to deal with the Nigerians than the Congolese. He will not get involved, not for a million rands. Life is good when one does not have to watch one's back nor fear for their family. He consults his watch then gets off his seat. He goes to grab a cup of coffee. Soon it will be time to bury himself in some paperwork.

Chike and Osas head straight to the club. They are buzzed into Papi's office. Inside the office, Ruth perches on the desk, cross-legged, leaving much of her plump thighs exposed. Rolls of currency notes held in place by rubber bands are heaped on one side of the desk. She sorts them into neat bundles.

Papi grunts in reply to their greeting, hardly looking up from the calculator in front of him.

"How the matter go?" he asks through the cigar held between his teeth.

"E no too go well, boss," Chike replies.

Papi looks up from the calculator.

"Wetin happen?"

"The pastor yarn anyhow. Na so we light am."

Papi looks from Chike to Osas. His face is devoid of emotions. "Which of una light the man?"

Chike is hesitant. "Na Osas."

Papi treats Osas to a lengthy stare. Osas meets the stare only briefly. "Boss, the pastor been dey talk say we dey work for boss wey no go school. Him no get respect for you. I no fit allow am go free as him dey mis-yarn just like that."

Papi's face softens. "Anybody see una?"

""No, boss. Nobody see us."

"Una sure?"

"We dey very sure."

"I no like say this kind thing dey happen now but make una dey very careful. I no want any heat this period, because I no ready to lose money."

They both nod in understanding. Papi waves them away, but when they get to the door, he calls back Chike. Turning to Ruth, he asks her to give him a private moment. He spanks her butt as she gets off and leaves.

"Sidon," he says to Chike.

Chike obliges, wondering what it could be that Papi wants to discuss.

"Shebi your head dey ground based on wetin dey happen for street?"

"My head dey ground, boss."

"You dey follow up the matter on Shabalala?"

He is referring to a cocaine kingpin in Johannesburg who had a bad run with a Nigerian cartel based in Colombia, seeking to tap into the South African supply chain. Twice, Shabalala's car had been riddled with bullets on the streets of Johannesburg while pulling into a strip club. Each time, he had escaped without so much of a scratch. A month later, he was found cold dead, half-naked on his bedroom floor. The room had been turned over, showing signs of a vicious struggle between two or more people. There were no entry wounds or bruises on the corpse, no signs of forceful entry into his penthouse suite, either. The police are still at a loss, the autopsy results are yet to be made public.

Chike says he has been following up on the matter like everyone else.

"You think say na the Colombia people kill am?"

"Boss, make I tell you true, me sef I no just know. The matter confuse me."

"You no think say na jazz?"

"Boss, that kind Jazz go strong o."

Papi puts down his cigar on a cut-glass ashtray. "I hear say your village people hand strong for jazz."

The sudden turn of conversation takes Chike by surprise. He stutters a little. "E get people wey dey run am for my place."

"Na wetin I want. I want person wey him hand strong."

"We fit arrange am. But who go dey run things when you travel go Naija?"

"I no tell you say I dey enter Naija. Shebi you still get your niggas wey you dey run things with for Naija?"

"Yes, I get my niggers for Naija."

"Arrange with them. Bring the jazz man come here."

"Okay. I go begin the arrangement. When you want am?"

"Na sharp-sharp things. Street don turn military like this now."

"No wahala, boss."

"You fit dey go. When you meet Ruth for outside tell her to come inside."

""Okay, boss."

Chike leaves. A moment later, Ruth re-enters. There is a playful questioning look on her face.

"Why you dey look me like that na?" Papi asks.

She shrugs and laughs as she makes to return to her place on the desk. Papi is unbuckling his belt.

"Come this side come give me small sugar," he says.

She lets out a laugh and obediently walks over to him. She helps him undo his fly, and then she parts his legs and goes down on her knees between them.

The call with Papi has just ended. Big Maskotoe tosses the phone onto the empty passenger seat and slides the key into the ignition. Someone taps on the window. It is a Buccaneer, one of the men from the fight at the Jamz club. The man smiles at him, "Aiye man, abi?"

Moskotoe freezes and then reaches inside his jacket, but the Buccaneer whips out a gun and fires. Blood and brain matter splatter all over the car, mixing with pieces and shards of broken glass.

Members of the gang are gathered in Papi's office. It is late evening. Papi does not see Maskotoe amongst them.

"Where Maskotoe dey?" he barks at the men. "Him dey fuck ashawo?"

"I been dey call am, but him no dey pick my call," Chike reports.

"Call am again."

Chike puts a call through. There is a series of buzzes, and then silence.

"The bastard!" Papi swears, seething. He turns to Osas with a grimace. "Oh boy, you dey with the walkie-talkies?"

"Yes, boss."

"Every other thing dey set?" the big man asks, sweeping the men with a searching glance.

"Everything complete boss," Chike affirms.

"In that case, make we dey go. We no fit wait for that bastard Maskotoe."

Shrouded in the darkness of a moonless night, Osas peers through the grating on the walkway bridge to look down at the empty street below. For a long time, nothing happens moves except for a passing car every occasionally. He wonders if this was, in fact, the right street but then he sees it: a white van approaching in the distance. In a sudden rush of anxiety, he speaks into his walkie-talkie. "The motor don dey come. E don near my bridge."

The muffled voice on the other end replies, "Okay. Begin dey go, then."

Osas creeps out of his position and disappears into the darkness.

At the next bridge a few kilometres away, the giant Obomo is squatted at a high point on the sidewalk, staring far up the road. He can finally see the white plumbing van. He picks up his phone. "The van is here."

The game has begun.

Kayode watches from his hiding place behind a building, as Mboma throws spikes into the road. The driver does not see them and drives the van right over them. All four tires burst, and the surprised driver instinctively slams on the brakes. The driver and his escort look around, bewildered, and reach for their guns.

Mboma spots Kayode, who has momentarily shortly stepped out from behind the building to see where the truck has stopped.

"Holy shit!" Mboma curses, running back to Kunta, who is squatted behind a cement barricade. "Nigewian gang is here!" he shouts.

Chike hears the announcement. Swearing under his breath, realizing that the plan is ruined, he steps out of his hiding place at a building entrance with a drawn rifle. He rains shots at the van and runs for cover.

A bullet hits a wall just above where Mboma has ducked behind the barricade with Kunta. He panics. "What ze fuck!"

Crouched by a concrete barrier on the other side of the road, close to Kayode, is Papi. The big man watches in bewilderment as Chike ducks back for cover.

"Nna wetin happen?"

"The stupid French boys dey see Kayode!" Chike shouts over to Papi.

At that instant, Mboma and Kunta open fire.

Bullets spray the walls all around the Nigerians as they concealed themselves further under cover. Gunfire erupts from the truck windows at Kunta and Mboma, who fall flat to the pavement. In reverse gear, the van backs over the spikes and away from the scene on full throttle despite the flat tyres. Next to the shuddering driver, the security escort makes a frantic phone call.

Osas lays flat on the ground in an obscure position, behind a tree, watching the gun battle going on. He spots someone crouching past toward the intersection. It is the huge Obomo, coming back from scouting. Osas allows him to get ahead then follows him, keeping to the shadows.

Kunta and Mboma intermittently shoot across the road, hoping to scare away the Nigerians.

Checking the bullets he has left in his magazine, Kunta shouts at Mboma, "Where's Obomo?"

"I no know!"Mboma yells, adrenaline pumping. "He neva come back since the —" He screams in agony. A bullet has struck his exposed thigh, tearing through the flesh. "They got me!"

Papi knows he has hit someone. He hears the cry of agony from across the road. His next shot, he decides, is going to blast someone's brains. Kayode keeps firing even though he could not see anyone behind the barrier. Beside Papi, Chike's gun is jammed.

"*Keeife o,* wetin be dat?"

"My gun!" Chike pants, his forehead coated with perspiration. He looks over Papi's shoulder, "Boss, behind you!"

Papi spins round, just in time to see Obomo raising his 9mm to take aim. A gunshot goes off. Obomo, with shock in his eyes, crumples to the ground.

"Osas!" Papi gasps.

Wails of police sirens rent the air.

"Oya, make we comot from here," Papi orders. He is the first to run towards the getaway car.

Part 4

RECONCILIATION

As human beings, we have the most
extraordinary capacity for evil. We can perpetrate
some of the most horrendous atrocities.
— Desmond Tutu

DEATH RUSH

Chamai's apartment is in semi-darkness; the only illumination comes from a single candle near his mattress on the floor.

Suddenly, a loud and insistent knock rattles the door. Chamai grabs a knife from beside the candle and gets up. He looks through the peephole to find Chike standing outside looking around wildly. He opens the door and Chike stumbles in, knocking him off balance and sending the knife clattering to the floor.

"Lock that door, sharp!" Chike orders.

Chamai picks up the knife and straightens himself to face Chike.

"The door! Lock it!"

"You force your way into my apartment at this

time of the night, and order me around," Chamai speaks slowly, as though each word were an inviolable gift to Chike. "I think you should leave."

"Chamai, abeg just lock the door first. I no know whether them follow me," he pleads.

Chamai locks the door, keeping his eyes on the uninvited guest. "Who is after you? Why did you come here?"

Chike drops into a seat. "Calm down now. We no be friends again?"

"We've never been friends," Chamai says flatly.

"At least we dey do business together. Right?"

"That's not answering my question. Why are you here?"

Chike takes a deep breath, as though collecting his thoughts. "Some guys are after me. I no know wetin I do dem. Dem block me for outside as I dey enter my apartment. As I escape na your place first enter my mind."

"How did you find me?"

"Eh?"

"I don't remember ever telling you where I live."

Chike chuckles. "That one na small thing. Once I dey do business with person, I must find out where him dey stay."

Chamai stares long and hard at him.

"See, I don tire, make I just rest small abeg. I go comot first thing for morning."

Silence ensues. Chamai is making up his mind. "First thing."

Chike nods. "Abeg I wan drink water."

Chamai picks up the candle and reluctantly crosses into the kitchen where he takes a dirty glass from out of the sink. Fetching water from the tap, he pauses. He reaches under the sink and takes out a bottle of capsules. He snaps the pill in two, empties the powdery content into the glass, and stirs.

"Thank you, my guy," Chike says, taking the glass and draining it. "This water taste funny."

"It's tap water," Chamai says.

It happens faster than he expects, but it is fun watching Chike gag and retch. Chike vomits all over the floor, clutching his belly. His eyes look wild and surprised. There seems to be much on his mind, even as he fights to stay alive.

Chamai picks up the knife and, in one swift move, slits Chike's throat. Blood spurts out. Chike clutches his throat, protesting the rush of his own death. Chamai slashes again, across the back of Chamai's neck, more savagely than before. He does so, repeatedly, never stopping until Chike is lying still, like the bloody corpse of some badly slaughtered animal, his head a few inches away from his body.

THE TRASHCAN DEAL

The Francophone gang gather at the bar. All of them seethe with rage. The Nigerians had dealt them a heavy blow that night. They had shot and killed Obomo, whose corpse was now with the police. Mboma sits on a chair, anguish on his face and one of his legs wrapped in a bloodied bandage. The rest argue about what to do to the Nigerian boys, how they could retaliate, for Obomo's sake and to reclaim their honour.

"We got do someting!" one of them is shouting. "We can't let zis go."

"Who killed Obomo?"

"It waz all darks out ter, man. But it was suwely one of zempwicks, we gots to kill zem all!"Mbomba shouts from his chair.

"We lost zer score and one of our own. Why

ah we here sulking, instead of going out ter and leaving bullets in zeir damn skulls?" asks another Francophone.

"Easy, man," Kunta counsels. "I vant to get back at ze bastards as much as yoo all do, but fo one, we don know where zey live."

"I do."

The whole crew spin round to see Chamai stepping in through the entrance without care in the world.

"Who ah yoo?" Kunta demands.

"Someone who's going to help you get retribution," Chamai answers. "I killed Chike last night, one of these people you seek. Now the Nigerians will come for me."

The Francophones stare at Chamai, uncomprehendingly. Kunta, for one, is not sure he has heard right. "What?"

"I killed him," the Zimbabwean answers simply, speaking as though he had simply burst a balloon. "Because the Nigerians will come for me—I'm sure of that—I'm going to need your protection. Out there isn't safe anymore."

"How did yoo find us?"

"I asked around," Chamai replies. "You're going to give me the security I need, and I will supply you with what you want—the location of your enemies."

"And how sure are we zat ze Nigewians are not using yoo to lure us out, huh?"

"Send one of your boys to go to the trashcan outside. Tell him to go with his cell phone."

"Why?"

"Because he's got some pictures to take."

"Don fuck wit us, boy!"

"In the trashcan, you'll find Chike. What's left of him?"

"What?"

Kunta nods at one of his men, who dashes off.

"If yoo lying to us," Kunta says, stepping over to Chamai, "yoo be dead meat."

Chamai merely smiles, a lifeless smile.

The Francophone man returns, clutching his nose and looking sick. He nods at Kunta, shows him the picture that he has taken.

Kunta looks up from the picture at Chamai and smiles. "Yoo got yoself a deal."

18

LOVE WAR

Chamai is in the backseat of the car across the road in between two members of the Francophone gang. Kunta is at the wheel, Mbomba, pumped full of painkillers, beside him.

Chamai points up the road to the barbershop. "One of them runs the place," he says. "It shouldn't be hard to nail him."

One of the gangsters takes out his gun, cocks it and walks up the road. A second after he enters the salon, two gunshots go off.

Andre, having come out of the gym, strolls towards his apartment, headphones on and bobbing his head to the rap music on his phone. He does not hear the car driving slowly up behind him. He does not see the Francophone's hand thrust out through the car window, an automatic gun in hand. The bullets throw him violently against the building wall. The rap music keeps playing but Andre can no longer hears it.

In his gold Mercedes Benz down the street from the rundown bar that he knows is the headquarters of the Francophone gang, Papi sits watching with Osas and two other Nigerians. The big man is behind the wheel, Osas clutching a shotgun beside him. Osas and the two Nigerians climb out and sprint into the dimly lit bar. They are doing this for Maskotoe, who the cowards had murdered, and for Chike, who has gone missing and who they think is probably dead.

Kunta is seated at his usual place at the back of the bar, his arm wrapped round a busty girl, when the Nigerians storm the place.

"See one de!" One of the Nigerians shouts, pointing to the back of the bar.

Osas and the two other Nigerians release an explosion of fire in Kunta's direction, riddling the gangster and his girl with bullets.

Osas sees two men make a quick duck for a side exit. He and two other Nigerians launch after them.

As they dash outside, the men turn into a corner leading to a car park. One of the Nigerians points his gun at the scampering Mbomba, but Osas pulls his wrist down. Faint sounds of approaching sirens can be heard in the distance.

"Make we comot for here," Osas orders.

Papi drops off Osas and the other Nigerians before heading towards his residence. Returning to his club and office would be a mistake right now, and likely, a costly one. As Papi enters his Houghton neighbourhood with its high walls, he thinks about how to deal with Osas after he is finished routing out the Francophone competition. He has not forgotten, or even forgiven Osas, despite the boy saving his life. There is still a score to settle.

For a fleeting moment, he thinks of Chike and Maskotoe. Their loss weighs heavy on his mind. Both were dependable lieutenants. They were his best and most trusted men. The night had been a rough one. Right now, he looks forward to the serenity and isolation his home offers. He needs to think things through and decide the next course of action. A sigh of relief escapes him as he turns into his driveway.

Gunshots rain on his car—how dare they ambush him at his own home. Horrified, Papi changes gear and screeches out of the driveway in reverse, swerving sharply into the street. More gunshots rain on the car as he races down the street, escaping his assailants.

He laughs aloud. He had always known this day would come and he had prepared well for it – his car is bulletproof.

Ruth lies in bed, smoking a cigarette, her thoughts elsewhere.

Papi steps out of the shower in his undershorts, a towel around his neck. He sits on the edge of the bed. "Everybody wan kill Papi but them no fit! Them never jam!" he laughs aloud.

"No be everybody wan kill you," Ruth says.

"Na who remain?"

"Me I no want kill you."

Papi snorts. "Na your mouth dey talk. But wetin dey your heart?"

Ruth stares at him. "Wetin you mean?"

Papi laughs. "You no know say to sleep with another man na to kill your husband?"

She sits up, stubs out the cigarette. "First first,

na my boyfriend you be, you no be my husband. Secondly, which man I sleep with?"

"You no dey fuck Osas?"

Ruth is taken aback by the accusation, its suddenness. "How you go talk that kind thing?"

"See as you shock. You think say I no know?" Papi smiles.

Ruth laughs mirthlessly. "I don find who I go fuck I no see, na that pikin I go carry? Abeg think straight, abi na dis una war dey affect your brain?"

"Na question I ask you, Ruth; yes or no?"

"And I say capital, NO! I no know where all that one from take enter your head. That matter for police station, na lie him talk. I just help am cover-up. Na that one you dey keep for mind reach today?"

Papi studies her for a moment. "Make I take am say I believe you. I need sleep now. I go enter Cape Town for morning go dey till this heat die down." He throws the towel to the floor and settles into a comfortable position on the bed.

It is not long before he starts snoring.

Ruth gets off the bed, picks the towel off the floor and heads for the bathroom. She hangs the towel up and goes to the mirror to look at herself. There is a war going on. People she knows have been claimed by its conflict. She regards it all to be senseless. There is no point in war except for greed – pure greed. Papi is fleeing tomorrow. Osas is out there, unprotected, at the mercy of the Francophones. She ponders on this.

Osas!

His story synchronises effortlessly with hers. There is no point in latching on to the swaying wings of doubt any longer. He is who she believes he is. Her son. She had fucked him, as stupid and ignorant as she was. The hell! To make matters worse, there is a bloody war raging outside, and he is out there, exposed, unprotected and in the very thick of it.

She has to do something. If Papi makes it out of this war, Osas will die. She knows Papi. He never forgives. If however, the big man loses, the enemy would eliminate Osas. The thoughts make her shudder. She will try to save her son. There has to be a way to make that possible. There is always a way. She, of all people, knows that.

ONE CHANCE

In the darkness of his room, Chamai lies on the floor. It is still and quiet all around, except for the distant car speeding past on the streets below. He listens to the sound of his breath until he thinks he hears a thud of a door being shut in the hallway. It has to be the landlady. A banging follows on another door. It goes on and on. It must be some tenant defaulting on rent. For some reason, Chamai thinks the defaulting tenant will not answer. They do not. A rain of abuses follows. Chamai tries to pick out the words, but they are muffled. The landlady is infuriated and, as always, she threatens to sell off the building. She has been saying that of late. Chamai wonders if she truly means it.

He hears feet stomping. A door opens and shuts. A key turns loudly in a lock, and then there is absolute silence. The landlady must have returned to her apartment. He feels pity for whoever lives with her, a husband maybe, the person who would have to put up with her present state of fury. Not once, though, has he seen another human leave her apartment. Maybe she does not live with anyone, not even any children, no lovers either. Or perhaps she has a family—children, husband, friends and all. Maybe he just has never hung around long enough to notice.

He wonders what would have happened to him if he owed rent right now. Surely, she would have come bringing furiously on his door, and he doubts he would have been able to ignore her assault. The cash he had taken from the dead man's place had taken care of his rent and utilities for four months upfront. He had been able to buy himself some peace from the landlady. The day is not far when the cash will run out. What will he do when his little stash of cash runs out? Had the money been substantial, he would have returned to Zimbabwe and settled into a more organised and assured life. South Africa is no place for him. It has treated him badly, and there is that Nigerian, that bloody one, who is the very devil, assigned to push him over the edge and scorn everything that made him a human capable of nursing and pursuing a noble ambition. Yes, he will have to leave South Africa. He will go back to Zimbabwe as soon as he has the means to afford a future insulated from the hopelessness of Zimbabwe, from that hopelessness that had driven him into South Africa and its resident demons.

Thoughts of his mother and her farm come to his mind. He wonders what she has been up to lately. Then he lets out a sigh. No need. Life appears to have forgotten people like her. She has forgotten all about life, too. He will have to do something for her, to help her; he will have to try, at least. How? Should he take her for a check-up at the doctor's? Should he care?

A heavy sigh escapes his chest and, for the first time, his gaze becomes less distant—it focuses through the darkness to the ceiling. There is not much of the ceiling he can make out. He presses his fingers against his eyes to ease the strain in them, and then reaches for his phone. He has heard that people make money on dating sites; prostitutes arrange hook-ups with male customers, and people get dates there, too. There are gay dating sites as well.

There are too many sites like those on Google Play's store. Opting for Tinder, he signs up as a rent boy. He goes through his gallery for his most recent pictures and chooses for his profile picture one that he had taken in his bathroom. It is suggestive and shows off his torso and much of his hairy armpit. A message arrives almost immediately. The sender is a man, an Indian, addressing his as 'baby.' It makes him nauseous. He drops his phone on the floor and turns away from it. What has he become? He has turned into someone he no longer recognises.

His phone beeps. Another Tinder message. A man, still. South African. He wants to know him better. Another, yet another. Maybe he should follow them up, he thinks, get to know them and then kill them one by one in their homes. Then he can take whatever possessions he can and make off with them. It will give the police something to work on, and the news of a serial killer running loose will create some thrill in society. Besides, these men—his victims— are predators, and he would be doing the world a favour by weeding them out, one at a time.

The mild midday sun seeps in through a parting in the curtain, passes over the sleeping form on the bed and beams on a spot on the wall next to a framed photograph of Oprah Winfrey. It is one of five photographs of Oprah adorning the room. In one, she is standing with teenage schoolgirls, all South

African. Someone had told April that Oprah runs a school for girls in South Africa and ever since then, April has dreamed of meeting this icon of a woman, who she would like to become someday, if only the stars would align for her.

April stirs on the bed and stretches. A grunt and then a long yawn. She had been awake for long but had remained in bed. It is always like this at this time of day, especially when there are no special clients. It will be unthinkable trying to get to Osas. He will be busy and may let her calls go unanswered. Of late, he has been very busy, difficult to track, always dodging her enquiries about what he has been up to. Very secretive fellow he is, but she loves him still. He is just too good. She turns in the bed and kicks off her duvet, exposing her naked thighs. It always leaves her feeling this way, whenever she thinks of him. She can still feel his touch caressing her body, his hands cupping her breasts and kneading them, the things he does to her whenever he enters her. She slaps around the bed for her phone. With shaky hands, she swipes through her phone gallery for his photograph, which she had gotten off Facebook. His picture sends a tingle between her legs. She slides her fingers down to her vagina and begins to stroke her clitoris. A moan escapes her, and her eyelids droop shut of their own accord. Her stroking becomes more spirited and then she quivers all over such that the hand holding the phone goes limp and the phone falls to the bed. A certain calmness comes over her as she lies still. Everything feels light. She shuts her eyes to live the moment and allow her mind to drift.

She remembers her early days in South Africa, her first client who had fumbled so much with putting his wee little thing inside her and then not lasted even twenty seconds as soon as he had his way. She thought of the first time she had sent money home. It had been the very first money she had gotten when Madam Ruth paid the girls at the end of the week. The other girls had cajoled her and told her that people back home would begin to think she is getting money abroad too easily, that they will become lazy and demanding soon.

She thinks of the first time she was robbed. She had been with a client in his car. They were headed to his place. Some group of men had appeared out of nowhere as the man pulled over at a convenience store to buy condoms. They had robbed him of his car, taken her purse, and the man had ended up with a gash on his forehead.

She thinks of Nigeria, of her childhood, but then her mind refuses to drift away from the memory.

Even as she tries to wish it away, her mind keeps dwelling on it with stubborn determination.

Benin City has never changed. Definitely not for her. Everything remained the same since the days she was a child, over the years that came and went. This much she can tell hawking around the streets and getting confronted with sights that challenged her mind for explanations. There were times, many times, when she could not offer any explanations. Mostly she remained silent, observing rather than talking. People said she acted much older than her age, but she stayed silent, comfortable with being an observer.

Once she developed breasts, they observed her instead. She noticed how men looked at her. And even some women, too. Their eyes spoke the things their mouths did not say. When she bent over her tray of groundnuts to serve some customer, she always caught their eyes looking through the neckline of her dress at her breasts. Once a mechanic in soiled coveralls had touched her breasts and his colleagues had laughed loud and hard. Nothing was funny about it—she hated the man for touching her with his greasy hands. She hated his colleagues, too.

Peter had told her he loved her, that he wanted her to be his girlfriend. She thought she understood. He was the son of the woman who owned the restaurant two yards away. He would smuggle bits of meat to her. Sometimes he brought her chicken. She liked the fried ones more than the peppered ones. She liked him, too. He had kissed her one day. She did not like it, but she did not say anything, and he never kissed her again.

Peter left out of the blue. He never told her. He simply disappeared. She did not know who to ask. Many a time, she would walk past the restaurant hoping to spot him or get a hint of his whereabouts, but activities in the restaurant went on as normal, only without Peter lurking about or helping serve the customers. There were times when she wished she could walk up to Peter's mother and ask her, but her courage failed her. How could she even go about it? She began to settle into the reality of Peter's absence. Maybe he would come back. He could have gone on a holiday somewhere. He had been possibly sent to a boarding school. But months went by, and she never saw him. One morning, she saw Peter's mother and her salesgirls loading all their wares and furniture onto a waiting truck. Her heart broke.

She had gone hawking and returned in the

evening, but her money was gone. Her stepmother would not hear of it. It meant they would starve, she lamented loudly. When she reached for the broom propped against the wall, April fled. It was better, the infuriated woman shouted, it was better that left than get herself strangled by her bare hands. As night fell, April, scared to return home, had wandered about, cold and hungry. She thought of Peter. As she lay on the verandah of a shop that had closed for the night, scared to shut her eyes, a form hovered above her. She sat up, startled. It was a familiar face, the old watchman who lived in a shack on the street corner. They said he was a widower and had no children.

"What are you doing here?"He asked.

She told him. He looked compassionate and told her to come with him to his shack. It isn't safe out here, he told her. In his shack, he gave her some biscuits and water, replaced the sheets on his flattened small mattress. The food and warmth lulled her to sleep. It was the touch of the old man that wakened her shortly afterwards. It was still night and the old man was naked as he fondled her breasts. He panted as he did. She was scared. It was a paralyzing fear that kept her from screaming or doing anything. In the darkness, he found her nipple and put his mouth to it. Like a starving child, he sucked, rubbing his erect penis against her buttocks, and then he spilled his milk on her.

By morning, he pleaded with her to marry him. He told her he had some money in his village. She should elope with him, he begged. She fled back home to a distraught stepmother who had been up and about all night, looking for her. She told her everything, but by the time the police had gotten to his shack, the old man was gone.

Two days passed, and Osas still had not seen April. He sits at a bar, nursing a cocktail, which he hardly sips. The night has started well. So far, he has sold half his stash of cocaine and even though things have slowed, he is still hopeful. New customers might come in and give him the signal. Some girl walks in with a guy. They make towards the VIP section with its entrance guarded by two bouncers. Osas trains his eyes on them but they do not signal him. Looking at them walk away, the girl's hips reminds him of April. He dials her number twice, but his calls go unanswered. It makes him mad to think she is still working in spite of her pregnancy. Or could it be that she isn't pregnant? Is she using pregnancy to hold him to her? Girls do. He is aware of such antics. But why would April do this to him? It just does not make any sense. April did not seem like that kind of girl. Although he will not want to admit it, he knows she likes him very much. She loves him. Madam Ruth likes him, too, in a fond kind of way. Not like April.

He thinks about the pregnancy. For a fleeting moment he considers the possibility that April will want to terminate it. Would it be a good idea? No. It will not be. She should keep it. He is soon to be a father. The sound of it feels strange but thrilling. Then he catches himself midway; he has not thought of Madam Ruth and how she will take the news that one of her girls is pregnant. Hell's fury will be unleashed when she finds out he is the one for whom April has gotten pregnant. The fury of such a woman will be disastrous. What about April? What if she learns about the times he has had sex with Madam Ruth? How will she take it? Everything feels desperate, like the way he did many years ago, before he made up his mind to be initiated into a secret cult.

Those who have spent time in Benin City agree that it is as true as it is famed. Osas had lived there all his life, and he thought the world no different. It was as rough in the house, which he shared with his embittered grandmother as it was outside, where one must venture out to fight a battle against hunger. Each day came with a balance between uncertainty and hope, depending on which side of the bed one woke up.

Shortly after Osas turned twelve, he found work as a bus conductor, as a daily assurance against hunger. He would rise early, wash his face and head out for the motor park. There would be other boys his age, some much older, canvassing to work for the bus drivers. There were times when he would be unlucky to not be chosen by any of the drivers. Those days he would return home and sit glued in front of the 14-inch TV, watching Nollywood movies. He never missed buying Nollywood movie CDs, whenever he earned any wages, and had already gathered an enviable pile of them.

On one of his lucky days, with his wage in his pocket, Osas had stopped at the usual roadside stall where he bought CDs. The owner had to reduce the volume on the loudspeaker to hear him.

"Oga, which one be latest?" Osas had asked him.

"This ones na new films," the man replied, lifting off some pirated CDs from his makeshift shelf.

"You been don sell this one for me," he said,

putting down one from the lot. He held up another. "This one fit no sweet."

"But you go like am."

"Na only Pete Edochie face go make this one sweet, but I no like this other man. Him too dey force himself, but the thing no dey am for body."

"You go like am. Na me dey tell you," the man had assured Osas.

But Osas would not let himself be swayed. He put down the CD in question and paid for three others before he headed home with his new supply. After eating dinner, whatever it is his grandma might serve, he would watch the movies until he felt sleepy.

Few poles away from his compound, three boys his age accosted him. They asked to see what valuables he had on him. The sheer effrontery of the boys surprised him at first, but then quickly enraged him. There was no way he could let them intimidate him. They fought. He fought hard but they roughened him up too bad and made away with his wages. They took his movie CDs, too. But before his bruises ever healed, there was another such encounter and another. He began to dread walking around the neighbourhood, especially with money or anything remotely valuable.

A fellow conductor, Timothy, who was a year

older than him, asked him about his constant bruises and he had told him everything.

"Na cult boys," Timothy had said flatly. Them dey rass you because you no be anything."

Osas looked on, dumbfounded.

"Them no go stop to dey rass you."

"So wetin I go do?" Osas asked.

"You go join frat too."

"I no fit join those boys upon everything wey them don do me."

"Who talk say you go join them?"

"No be wetin you talk just now?"

"O boy, use your head. You go need join another frat wey no be their own. If you try join their own, na small boy you go be for them. You no go get any levels. Come join our frat. Those boys no go dey put eye for your matter again. If them try you again, make you know say my name no be Timothy."

Days had come and gone while Osas pondered on whether to join any fraternities. He hadn't known Timothy was a fraternity member, but it began to make sense as to why the boy was always bold and fearless. He could mobilize any number of boys, his members, whenever the need arose, and each one would fight dirty and bloody as though their lives depended on winning.

The longer Osas spent pondering, the more things got worse. And then, one day, he searched for Timothy, to tell him he was ready to accept his offer. Two days later, he was standing half-naked and blindfolded by the side of a river under a full moon. It was the night of his initiation into the most dreaded fraternity in Benin City.

April wakes up feeling nauseous. Her mouth tastes metallic, as though she has been fed some pot scrapings. She checks the time. 9:15 *am*. Unbelievable! She had gone to bed early and has slept for too many hours. She had only served two customers and then a third one had taken her to his hotel room. A gentleman, quite unsure of himself; perhaps a married man who was cautious of the nagging feeling that he wasn't doing right. He had not bargained with her. In his hotel room, he had felt much safer. After two rounds of hasty sex, he had paid her a little above their agreed rate and asked her to leave. These are the kind of men who would pay up if blackmailed, she had thought as she dressed and left the hotel. Maybe he had paid her extra to buy her silence. She had gone straight home afterwards because it was looking like the rest of the night would be unproductive.

She gets off the bed and pads towards the cramped bathroom with the rusty shower and faucets. Maybe she will feel much better after she brushes her teeth. She turns on the faucet and lets the tap run as she presses toothpaste onto her toothbrush. She hadn't started brushing when she hunches forward, retching. There is nothing in her stomach. All what she throws up is some slimy fluid that looks like whipped egg yolk. She rinses her mouth and holds onto the faucet to keep steady. Her head spins. She feels light, as though she will be swept away, if a gust of wind were to blow into the bathroom through the small window.

What can possibly be wrong with her? She doesn't want to pay heed to the answer that pops up in her mind. No, it's not an answer. It is just a suggestion being conjured by her mind. But she doesn't like it, doesn't want to entertain the thought. She can't be pregnant. But what if? What if she is pregnant? Osas must be responsible for the pregnancy. She never has sex without condoms. Madam Ruth had warned against anyone giving in to the pressures of unprotected sex, no matter the monetary incentives.

HIV is like MTN recharge cards here, she had warned, they just hand it to you, very easily.

She waves the train of thought away from her mind. It is too early in the day to entertain such negativity. She gets ready, thinking about what to wear even as she showers. It is to the hospital she will go, first, to be sure that everything is okay.

The waiting room of Helen Joseph Hospital is full this morning. Hardly any of thepadded seats are vacant for long before someone comes in and sits down. The woman seated next to her is looking like she is cast in stone. On the other side of her is a younger girl, seated crossed-legged and busy with her iPhone. On the seat across, a voluptuous woman in a print dress and a scarf around her head casts her discomfiting stare. Next to the woman is a sullen-looking teenage girl, obviously her daughter. April meets the woman's stare, but only briefly and then looks away. She hopes there will be a vacant seat elsewhere, so she can stay away from the woman's stare, which reminds her of her witchy kind in Benin City.

A nurse walks into the waiting room, a writing pad in hand. She calls out April's name. It's her turn to go pick up her test results. She walks into the designated office. There is an elderly uniformed staff nurse seated behind a desk. Her bespectacled face is blank, devoid of any emotions.

"You're April Okojie?" she asks, never looking up from an open notebook before her.

"Yes, ma."

She hands April a sealed envelope, turns the notebook around, and shoves it towards her. "Sign in the space against your name."

"Please give me your pen."

She hands April a pen from the table, looking at her above the rims of her spectacles. April appends her signature, and then leaves the office. Outside, she tears open the envelope with shaky hands. Her gaze flies across the paper and then she sees it. *Positive.* She's pregnant! God! She shoves the paper and envelope into her handbag and begins to walk, ignoring a honking taxi anticipating her patronage. She needs to expend the nervous energy while she sorts things out in her head.

It is just a month's pregnancy; the test results have said. How will Osas take it? Or should she not tell him? No, she will have to. But how does she get to meet him? He no longer stays at Chike's place and she doesn't know where he is presently located.

She walks into an eatery and settles at a table

next to the glass paneling. Getting out her phone, she dials Osas' number. He doesn't reply the first time. Not the second time either. Obviously, he is busy at the moment. She will have to get the message across to him somehow. He deserves to know. If he doesn't want the pregnancy, she will abort it. She composes a text, hesitates over it, hits *send* and breathes a sigh of relief. Looking up, she sees a uniformed waitress standing over her, a practiced smile plastered on her face.

"Get me some tea. And some doughnuts too," she says.

Sunday often leaves Ruth with very little to do. She never went to church and would remain in bed far into the morning, finding something to occupy herself with for the rest of the day until evening, when she would go see her girls and how they were faring on the streets. Evenings were always the salvation of Sundays for her.

This particular Sunday is no different. She has slept until eleven in the morning and then she goes to treat herself to a lengthy hot shower. Her phone on the bed rings. The caller will have to wait, she says to herself. It won't be too important. Another round of ringing follows after the first, but she continues with her shower, unperturbed.

Finally, she turns off the shower and walks naked into the bedroom, toweling her body as she does. She does not go for the phone yet but walks over to her wardrobe and throws the doors open. Inside, from a box of clothes, she pulls out a small opaque bottle. The sangoma had given it to her on her second visit. Uncorking the bottle with care, she pours some liquid on her palm, rubs them together and dabs at her forehead, arms and feet. She also dabs some of it on her head. Satisfied, she returns to bottle to its secret place and then goes to the phone. Two missed calls. It is Esther, one of her girls. She hopes nothing is wrong as she dials Esther's number.

The phone is answered at once. Esther greets her. She wants to know if she is home as she is in the neighbourhood and wants her audience. It is important, she says. Ruth tells her to come at once. Good girl, she says as she puts down the phone; she has the good sense to call first before knocking on her door. She throws a bathrobe over her body, lights a cigarette and takes up position in front of a dressing mirror.

As she lines her eyebrows, there is a knock the door, a timid one. As Esther enters, Ruth can't help noticing her air of reverence.

"Good morning, ma."

""Ehe, you don come? Wetin be the matter wey no fit wait until evening?"

Ma," she sounds hesitant. Ruth pauses her makeup and stares at her through the mirror. "Na April, ma.

"Wetin do April? She come back last night at all?"

"Yes, ma. She come back. The thing be say she no well."

"Wetin do her?"

"Madam, I no know, but the way I carry dey see am, e be like say she don carry belle."

Ruth turns around in her seat to look at Esther. "Na she carry her mouth tell you so?"

"No o. She no tell me anything. She only tell me say na just small sickness. But me I no be small pikin. I don carry eye look am I know wetin I dey see."

"Okay. I don hear you. Shebi she dey house?"

"Yes. She dey sleep when I comot for house."

"Okay. E get another thing you want tell me?"

"No, ma."

"Okay. We go see for evening."

"Thank you, ma."

Esther opens the door and leaves. Ruth continues with her makeup even as she wonders how the girl could become so stupid. Has she not given every one of them enough orientation on running the streets safe? Who knows if it isn't more than pregnancy? HIV? Or some malicious STD? Why would some girl with a future trifle with her life so? But then what if it wasn't only April? What if some of her other girls are flouting the rules, too, and being careless? She won't let that happen. The girls still owed her. They would first offset their debts, then they could be as careless as they want. It won't be her business any longer. But at the moment, she will have to straighten April out. If the girl has fallen in love with some man, as the stupid ones do, and if the man is rich enough to pay off the girl's debts, then everyone will be fine. She would let the girl go. Otherwise, nobody walks away until their debts are settled.

Two hours later, Ruth is seated on a park bench. She waits for April. Anyone could pass her by at that moment and not recognize her as the proprietress of the Nigerian prostitution ring in Braamfontein. She looks strikingly different in her sweatshirt and pants. Her sneakers lend her a more mellow and youthful disposition. Her hair is packed into a woollen cap and she is wearing mild makeup.

April doesn't arrive until a good thirty minutes later.

"Good morning, ma," she greets Ruth.

"Na afternoon be this," Ruth corrects. "Wetin make you delay?"

"Ma, I beg no vex. I no see taxi on time."

"Okay." She pats the space next to her, an indication for April to take a seat. April obeys, keeping as much space between them as is practical.

"How your body?"

"I dey fine, ma."

Ruth stares at her, focusing on her breasts and looking out for all the tell-tale signs of early pregnancy. "Wetin them talk say dey do you?"

"Nothing o," she says, her voice rising in defense. But then she reads into the heightened suspicion on the older woman's countenance. "Na just night fever I dey get."

"Shebi I tell una say make una no dey fuck raw?"

"Ma?"

"Keep quiet for there! Una no dey want hear word. No be to only get breast and toto make you woman. You suppose get sense too. How we take know say you never get HIV join the belle wey you don carry?"

"Ma, I no carry HIV. I sure for that one."

"We dey go check you like this now. After we finish, we go comot the belle."

"Madam, I beg, give me small time. I need tell the person wey get the belle before anything."

"Oh. Thank God say you sabi am. Who him be? I hope say no be all this yeye SA men or one Maputo person. If na them, na time you dey waste for me here so."

"No, no be SA man. Na Naija person."

"You dey mad? Wetin dey worry you? Naija person na him ashawo go carry belle for? Na one chance you dey so. Who be this person? I go sabi am?"

"Madam, na Osas."

"Who?" Ruth asks, unsure if she heard correctly.

"Osas. Na one of Papi boy."

Ruth looks as if she'd been struck by lightning.

April can't help notice, and she grows scared. "Madam, I beg, I love am."

"Shut up! Just shut up."

April falls silent.

"You talk say him no know?"

"I send am text. I suppose meet am make we talk."

"You go dey go house now. I go handle the matter."

"Okay, ma."

April gets up and walks away, glad to escape a situation that had grown tense and confrontational. Ruth remains seated on the bench. The world seems to be closing in on her. She can't tell exactly if it is jealousy or indignation that she feels. But whatever it is, it stabs at her heart and threatens to cut off her breath.

COSMIC CONFESSION

Detectives Jiba and Booysen are driving slowly along the backstreets of Braamfontein in an unmarked vehicle. The news of the gang war is thick in the air. A special taskforce has been hastily set up with all police resources made available to it. Restoring stability in the area has become top priority, as there are fears that things might escalate with reprisal attacks among rival gangs.

Jiba is behind the wheel. Besides him, Booysen listens to him talk about the wrong type of immigrants making the country uninhabitable for everybody. He believes Jiba is right. So much his partner is saying adds up, even though he has not seen things from his perspective before. There is a lot of work to be done and so much of it rests with Immigrations. What are the politicians even doing about this?

Something catches Booysen's attention at an adjoining street separated from them by the concrete island. He draws Jiba's attention to it.

Osas is running across a side street and a Francophone gangster is in determined pursuit, Chamai trying to keep up behind them.

"Call for backup!" Jiba shouts, stepping down on the accelerator. "We're getting these sons of bitches for good."

Osas turns into another street and keeps running but he can feel his legs getting weaker. The exhaustion is getting to him. He knows it is only a matter of time and the Francophones will get him. He races down another street and spots a space between two buildings. Without a moment's hesitation, he runs into it, out of breath, unsure of where it leads to. All that matters is to keep going if he is to put off his impending fate. A plank unexpectedly hits him behind his legs, and he trips, his feet tumbling out from under him. A few meters away is a barbed wire fence.

Osas makes to stand and keep going, but one of the Francophone gangsters is on top of him and delivers a savage punch to his ribs. Chamai catches up at that instant. He delivers a kick directly into

Osas' groin. The pain is explosive. Osas crumples into a ball.

The Francophone gangster takes out a gun and points it at him. "Now what, pwick?"

Detectives Jiba and Booysen come running up the small alley behind them.

"Police! Put down your weapon!" Booysen shouts.

The Francophone gangster spins round, gun in hand.

On impulse, both detectives fire a series of shots. The gangster takes most of the bullets to the chest. He staggers two steps backward and crumbles to the ground next to Osas. Chamai looks from the gun lying on the pavement to the two detectives.

The detectives train their guns at him. "Don't move!"

Chamai takes a step towards the gun and detective Jiba fires a warning shot into the air. Chamai gives up reaching for the gun. He turns to the detectives instead. "These people turned me into a monster!" he screams at them. "I came here to make a better life for myself. But all there is here for people like me is pain and suffering and horror!"

Both detectives' glance at one another, confused by the strange and sudden outburst of emotion from the young man who doesn't look any bit a gangster. Chamai starts crying, tears streaming down his face. Osas begins wriggling his way slowly towards a small gap in the barbed wire fence.

"Just put your hands on your head and we can talk about this calmly," Detective Jiba tells Chamai.

But Chamai begins pacing up and down instead, disoriented. He comes to a standstill and turns to the detectives again. "I killed them," he says, almost inaudibly. And then louder. "I killed them! All those men! I slit their throats! I smashed their heads in!"

Booysen edges closer, his partner spreading out to his side.

"You need to tell us what happened," Booysen says "We need to hear your side of the story. What's your name?"

Chamai regards the both of them for a moment, and then, without any warning, reaches for the gun.

"Don't do it!" Booysen screams, his finger on his gun's trigger.

Chamai puts the barrel to the roof of his mouth and presses the trigger. Both detectives flinch as the gun goes off. They look on, aghast, at the boy's corpse, as it crumples like a ragged doll to the ground. Booysen turns away, doubles over and pukes. While the detectives had their attention on Chamai, Osas had been crawling the hole in the fence. He slips through and begins to inch away.

"Stop right there!" Jiba shouts, taking aim.

"Let him go," Booysen says, standing up and looking drained. "We have had enough deaths for one day.

Papi drives along the highway, glancing worriedly at his speedometer. He can't wait to get out of the hellhole that has become of Braamfontein and find refuge in Cape Town. His connections there will help him disappear for a while. From Cape Town, he can continue strategizing. Perhaps a little advice from his counterparts wouldn't be a bad idea. And Osas, he hoped the Francophones had gotten to him. One thing about the Francophone boys is that they are merciless killers. He hopes they had done their job and saved him the trouble of weeding out the boy himself.

A sudden pain sears through his lower abdomen. It feels like a knife has cut through his intestines. He frowns. Did he eat something bad? He takes one hand off the steering wheel and clutches his stomach. The pain comes again, worse than the first time. Slowing down, he brings the car to a stop on the side of the highway. The pain comes again, this time making him nauseous. His head swoons. He retches blood. He feels a warm wetness trickle out of his nostrils. Wiping his nose, he looks at his hand. Blood. Alarm shoots through his mind. He makes to reach for his phone but for some reason his body seems not to pay him any need. It dawns on him that he is losing control of his muscles. His body is shutting down! There can only be one explanation: Ruth. She had served him tea and a plate of toast and egg that morning in bed. The tea had a slightly odd taste, but Ruth had soothed his worries, saying it was Indian Masala tea. Ruth had walked him to the door and kissed him on the forehead. The kiss of death! The filthy whore had poisoned him. Why? Had a rival gang paid her off? Why would Ruth betray him? They were business partners who helped each other make a fortune, so why? Because she is fucking that boy? It has to be it! Osas!

Papi sinks into oblivion. His head drops onto the steering wheel, sending the horn into an unceasing wail, his unseeing eyes open and spittle and blood dribbling from his face.

The only place that Osas can think of is Ruth's brothel. He is bleeding. His clothes are torn and dirty, and he is attracting too much attention on the streets. He is also short on cash. Perhaps, he thinks to himself, Ruth would be able to clean him up and give him enough money for him to go into exile. This place is not safe for him anymore. Where is Papi? He had been on his way to report to Papi's office when the enemy had found him. If those police officers had not come in time, he would have been a corpse, lying in the open and getting cold. Who was that other boy? Shot himself in the head like that! What was it he said to the police officers about being a serial killer? A boy? How could that be?

He staggers through the back door of the brothel. He is in the corridor when he hears her voice and stops in his stride.

"After them kill Angela, all of una been dey lament," Ruth is saying to her girls in the lounge area. "Make I talk my own story before una come think say na una own bad pass. See, make I tell una. Noting una don see wey I never see times two."

Unseen, Osas listens closely. He had never thought to ask Ruth her story. This was his chance of getting to hear it.

"I been dey eighteen years old for Benin when my grandmama, Mama Cecilia, collect my baby boy, carry me sell give Babel James for two thousand. Them carry me go shrine, cut hair from my toto."

Osas's heart skips a beat. Mama Cecilia? His grandmother?

"I follow drink," Ruth goes on. "I follow swear. No be these days wey some of una dey see plane ticket. Babel James carry me come here. Him show me shege but I use my toto free myself. Now I be big madam. But each time I think about my pikin wey I leave for Benin, my Omorogie, I be wan cry..."

Osas has heard enough. In a daze, he enters Ruth's office in unsteady steps. He finds a few hundred rands in her handbag and shoves it in his pocket. Once back in the streets, he flags down a cab and calls his destination to the driver. He settles into the backseat, leans back and shuts his eyes to every sight.

Ruth's words buzz around his mind. How could this have happened to him? Madam Ruth, his mother? Her words tumble on his mind like a barrage. They refuse to be kept at bay, even as the taxi drops him at the train station and he pays his fare. Even as he washes himself in the bathroom. Even as he buys a new pair of jeans and a T-shirt and pays for a ticket to a destination he does not even know. The train is about to leave the station and he simply wants to get on it. Osas knows he will spend the rest of his life struggling with the things he had heard Ruth say. They are agonising and they promise to weigh heavy on his spirit far into the future.

Sitting by the window of his cabin, he watches the receeding city of Johannesburg as the train gathers speed. He wishes he could somehow turn back time and redo everything. It is a vain wish. He is stuck with this broken reality, on a train bound for an unknown destination. Oghogho running away from him through the crowd back home in Nigeria comes to mind again; a ghostly image that, like Ruth's confession, will never leave him alone. All that matters now is that he has escaped Braamfontein and all its strangers.

There is peace in the hope of flight, but not in new beginnings.

END

ACKNOWLEDGEMENTS

I read Chika Unigwe's *On Black Sisters' Street* when it was published. Then, it inspired the screenplay of a film that I wanted to shoot in Italy, working with Kuby Uyanga. After a year, travelling to Milan, to meet executives of MediaSet, who were not willing to fund the project, I decided to novelise it and South Africa – which is the most developed country in Africa – is the only place I could set this story, as it is where all Africans want to move to.

I thank:

Olisa Eloka, who helped me work on it. And Cheta Igbokwe, my assistant, whose dedication reflects in how it all happened.

Jeremy Warren Rourke worked tirelessly in shaping up the narrative. Mmamello Matake read it in manuscript and gave me a go-ahead. It was then, that Somak Ghoshal took his time to edit it.

Ikenna Chinedu Okeh, my brother, my first reader, for helping to navigate through the streets of Braamfontein, for the input.

Nobel Laureate, Wole Soyinka, who read my manuscript, encouraged me and even said it read like a film, without knowing that it was first written for film. He also asked for a cameo appearance if ever made into a film.

Dr. David Pratten of African Studies Centre at Oxford University, for his kindness and support.

Japheth Omojuwa, for being the big brother and inspiration. And Tolu Ogunlesi, my brother. For everything.

Akeem Ibrahim, for doing all the hard work. God bless you!

Okechukwu Chukwuocha, my brother, who will always come through for me. Anytime. May the heavens keep you and your family.

Professor Henry Louis Gates Jr, for creating time to host me in Harvard, for shouting my name before anyone else.

James Currey read it. And loved it!

Priya Doraswamy, the most dedicated agent I have had. Passionate. Fervent. Mercurial. Sedulous. Driven and persevering.

Debbie Edwards, my manager, the one with compassion, gentleness, leniency and warmth. For everything you have done for me. Keep flying.

Robert Greer, Ashton Bainbridge, Emma Mitchell, Kealey Rigden and everyone at FMCM for embracing me. Fully to create an everlasting beauty. I thank you all.

Julie Mabey, of One World Publications. Kind-hearted. Generous soul. May God bless you!

Thank you very much, Pelagie Okorie and Salma Idris, for everything. For all the joy that you bring.

My dearest Michael Ogah, for the friendship of many years. For always creating time to read my manuscripts. For Jon Ogah, for hosting me in Grenoble and Patrick Ogah, for being my warrior.

Thabiso Mahlape, my energetic and assiduous South African publisher at BlackBird Books, who drove that beautiful afternoon to have lunch and talk about my future. And Thandeka Ncube, whose email that morning in Sao Paulo, brightened the whole day and got me partying. Tolu Daniel's attention to details and delicate notes, helped refine this book as my editor.

Bibi Ukonu, my Canadian publisher, for being studious and unflagging. And everyone at Griots Lounge Publishing, for believing in this dream. Kara Toews, for her suggestions and edit, and also understanding that Pidgin English is a special language.

Special thanks to Echezonachukwu Nduka, for the time spent, reading and editing and making beautiful comments on the characters.

Bankole Olayebi, my Nigerian publisher at BookCraft Africa, most conscientious, for that phone call, which got me brimming. For putting me on an 'elitist list.'

Thanks to Ogala Osoka, for working on the edit with me.

Adejoke Oyekan of BookCraft Africa, for her efficiency and warmth.

Uzor Maxim Uzoatu, my editor at Abibiman Publishing UK, for giving all his time to it. Thanks to Antoinette Isama, my editor at Abibiman Publishing US and Professor Akachi Ezeigbo, for everything.

Thanks to Obi Odenigbo, Commissioning Editor at Abibiman Publishing, for the hospitality when I visited him in Cedar Rapids and for everything.

Most grateful to Fiona Marsh of Midas PR, for all the hardwork.

The other publishers I don't know yet.

My sister, Nkechi Nwelue, spent a lot of money and resources on this project. Then, my brother, Odinaka Nwelue, who read the manuscript and made some input, while playing host to me in his large apartment in Budapest, on my return from Milan. My other brothers, Chijioke Nwelue, Ebere Nwelue and Ifeanyi Nwelue, came through in their own ways.

Derby Milano, for taking a ride to Milan to be with me, for the laughter and for the love, while meeting MediaSet. Okwuchi Uzosike called from London and asked that whatever I ate in the Nigerian restaurant was to be left for him to pay. His cousin, Chinonso "Harry" Madu, stayed by myself, supportive.

Dr. Giovanni Altieri of MediaSet for being a great host in Milan. Thank you, Pietro Collini, for making the connection and I remain grateful to Mr. Altieri's assistant, Valentina Lerone.

Roberta Gioncada, my beautiful and kind friend, for all the happiness and joy you bring to my life.

Ugochukwu "TerryTheVoice" Odenigbo, great guy, great supporter, great travel companion. Thanks to Obinna Odenigbo, the man with the finest voice, who never says no to me.

Chudie Igweonu, top guy, great company, old friend!

Ejiro Onobrakpor and Ogeh Cynthia, my Calgary people, for everything.

Ndukwe Eleanya, Raymond Haastrup, Mbong

Amata, Cornell Sewell, Mohamed Dione and Luis Lopez, my indulgent, good-natured and kind-hearted Hollywood team; for creating time anytime I am in California, to take care of me, doting me and being completely benign. There was that evening that Leila Djansi prepared fufu with goat meat soup for me and Mohamed. Thank you!

Auntie Nkechi Obiora, my defender, supporter and cheerleader, who always reminds me of my mother, for standing for me in my absence, when my cousin, Ade Ladejobi 'trashed' me. For driving all the way from New York to Newark to attend my film screening at Newark Film Festival. This is to thank the Obioras, beginning from Auntie Ngozi, Auntie Alex, Auntie Juliet, Auntie Esther, Uncle Noel to Uncle George – for the little things that matter.

Ifeanyi Ebuka "Jacksparrow" Iloegbunam, best friend, personal soldier, rock, with whom, I am never afraid of being locked up – he will always come through and sign a surety, for the police to release me, when I get arrested.

Seun Kuti, friend and brother, for always checking up on me, to make sure I am alive.

And to my hero, Kunle Afolayan, for treating me as a true protégé.

Kemi Adetiba, my inspiration, my muse, my cheerleader.

Mitterand Okorie, for the solid friendship, for the gossip and for supporting me and cheering me, even when he knows things are hard. For everything.

Tochi Nwokeafor, who will run out and leave everything he is doing, when I am in Accra. And Ugochukwu Nwolisa, my darling friend.

Gabriel Adeyemo, restless soul, kindhearted, for being my pillar. For all the enjoyment he brings to life.

My father, Sam, who encouraged me to write very early in life. He never stopped supporting me. And my mother, Ona, reads all my manuscripts before anyone else.

Auntie Jane Uneanya, my "Ohio mother," for taking care of my parents, while I went round the world.

Ibrahim Huthman, my rock, my brother – I owe him a lot of money and I won't forget how he cared for me. And Godswill Ugwuamaka, who will always support and never says no to me.

Dr. Negash Ghirmai, who was kind enough to let me into Ohio University. And it wouldn't have been possible to meet him, without the love of Professor

Amritjit Singh, for everything, beginning from Hyderabad.

Professor Zakes Mda, for the afternoons in Athens and the evenings in Johannesburg. Great teacher.

Bose Maposa and Keith Phetlhe, made my stay in Athens worthwhile. Thank you!

Chigozie Obioma, dear friend, supporter, for encouraging me to focus on this particular book.

Professor Sikhumbuzo Mngadi, for every help rendered. For the opportunity. And to everyone at the University of Johannesburg, who supported me.

Adeleke "Leke" Togun, on the trip to Cape Verde, cooked for me, every morning and would ask: "Do you need anything?" He did this, while I wrote or read or just sat, animatedly.

These Ambassadors to Nigeria, supported me greatly, making things easy for me to travel: His Excellencies, AR Ghanashyam (India), Bobby Moroe (South Africa), Stuart W Symington (the United States), Paul Arkwright (the United Kingdom), Esmond St. C Reid (Jamaica), BN Reddy (India), Tobern Getterman (Denmark), Alejandro Garcia Moreno Elizondo (Mexico) Jens-Petter Kjemprud (Norway), James Christoff (Canada), Mary Beth Leonard and many others.

Consul General Darkey Africa, thank you! Thank you to Aruna Amirthanayam, Larry Socha, Hideki Sakamoto.

Miko Yamanouchi, strong bird, strong wings, strong soul. Thank you for everything!

Tolu Akanni, Ikenna Aniekwe, Agu Tochukwu, Jude Idada, Joseph Ogunniyi, Ifeanyi Orazulike, Yinka Bode-George, my Toronto squad, who will drop everything they are doing and come see me when I am in their territory.

Jake Okechukwu Effoduh, my lawyer, my friend and everyone at Praxis and Gnosis.

Ayodele Arigbabu, my first publisher, my pillar, my bag of wisdom, for never ever letting me down.

Jahman Anikulapo, for raising me and for never giving up on me. Thank you to Aderemi Adegbite, for giving me shelter and food and love. Thank you, to Deji Toye, Ropo Ewenla, Folu Agoi, Edaoto and Mr. Toyin Akinosho.

Godmother Molara Wood, for the love, kindness and encouragement to become better. And Jude Dibia, for everything.

Hilda Dlamini of Home Affairs, for ever being supportive. And Mr. Adziliwi Muravha and Mr. Stephen Mabasa, for all the support.

Magnus Amudi, Jide Sowemimo, Dudley

O'Shaughnessy, Chinedu Ohiaeri, Fred Martins, PS Quint, Ishaya Bako, Kolawole Olajide, Uti Nwachukwu, Denrele Edun, Adekunle Owolabi, Dan Akinlolu, Pinkie Megkwe, Timothy Anyanwu, Kelvin Alisi, Tonye Altraide, Lorenzo Menakaya, Alfred Odiba, Blessing Uzzi, Torkuma "TK-Swag" Nyior, Anthony "Tkinzy" Felix, Mishael Maro Amos, Duncan Ifijeh, Jude Chima Ndu, Obinna Oti, Hymar David, Javier Gutierrez Lozano, Arun Jay, Namita Gokhale, Mita Kapur, Solomon Elusoji, Sonye Allanah, Aniche Christian, Osondu Awaraka, Eromo Egbejule, Uzoukwu Nzeribe, Oluchukwu Chukwunyere Benneth, Nzeji Bethel Francis, Siyabonga Mbaba, Elvis Sekhaolelo, Obinna Obika, Chidinma Akaniro, Chioma Amaryllis, Okechukwu Chukwuocha, Oluyinka George, Obinna Isaac, Damian Eguji, Kennedy Ekezie, Bella Ndubuisi, Japheth Omojuwa, Sophie Bouillon, Nwaka Nnamdi, Joshua Darlington, Dozie Ejiofor and Auntie Ejine Nzeribe, for all the love and support.

Earl Lovelace, for that lunch, for the listening ear, for the hospitality in his serene home in Port of Spain. Thanks to Asha Lovelace, for her kindness, hospitality and taking good care of me when I was in Trinidad.

Aboyeji "E" Iyinoluwa – my brother and kindred spirit. Always looking out for me. Thank you!

Colonel Shakes Mashalaba of the High Commission of South Africa in Abuja, for the meekness and diffidence. Such a great soul.

Chief Chidebem Nwaebube – the Chief of Braamfontein, who saw me through school. And Chief Uche Nworah, who has never stopped supporting me.

Shobhaa De, my soul-mother, the best out there, the one wrapped in humility. Thank you for always supporting.

Arundhati Roy, who has the strong ability to understand and share the feelings of others. Thank you for letting me into your home and life.

To whom ever that will be in a relationship with me; thank you for not showing up. Thank you for giving me time to write this book.

And thanks to those I couldn't write their names here. I have more books and I will create space for that.

Daalụ